BELIEVE IN ME

SIERRA CARTWRIGHT

HAWKEYE

BELIEVE IN ME

Copyright @ 2021 Sierra Cartwright

First E-book Publication: November 2021

Editing by GG Royale

Proofing by Bev Albin and Cassie Hess-Dean

Layout Design by Once Upon An Alpha

Cover Design by Once Upon An Alpha

Photo provided by Depositphotos.com

Promotion by Once Upon An Alpha, Shannon Hunt

All rights reserved. Except for use in a review, no part of this publication may be reproduced, distributed, or transmitted in any form, or by any means, electronic or mechanical, including photocopying, recording, or by any information storage and retrieval system, without prior written permission of the author.

This is a work of fiction. Names, characters, places, brands, media, and incidents are either the products of the author's imagination or are used fictitiously, and any resemblance to any actual persons, living or dead, is entirely coincidental.

The author acknowledges the trademarked status and trademark owners of various products referenced in this work of fiction. The publication/use of these trademarks is not authorized, associated with, or sponsored by the trademark owners.

Adult Reading Material

Disclaimer: This work of fiction is for mature (18+) audiences only and contains strong sexual content and situations.

It is a standalone with my guarantee of satisfying happily ever after.

All rights reserved.

DEDICATION

*Shayla, your friendship is an amazing gift. I'm blessed.
Seester, you are the absolute best. How did I get so lucky?
Always for Melinda Parker, BAB, Linda Pantlin Dunn, Susan
Bayliss, Angie Foster, and Gayla O'Dell*

PROLOGUE

HAWKEYE

Getting a ping at four-thirty a.m., before the coffeemaker had finished hissing out its life-sustaining caffeine, should be illegal. Unfortunately for protective agent Garrett Young, it was an occupational hazard.

As he grabbed an oversize mug from the cupboard, he opened his secure texting service.

Shit. The message was from Hawkeye, the owner of the security firm where Garrett worked. Hearing from the boss himself was never good. And no doubt it meant Garrett wouldn't be on his noon flight to Cozumel for a much-needed week of diving, sunshine, sand, and beer.

Got a job.

A second missive followed.

The diner. 0600.

Once he'd typed out his affirmative reply, Garrett lasered in on the routine he maintained to keep himself sharp and focused. After downing a cup of coffee, he headed to his in-home gym for some resistance training, followed by sweat-inducing cardio. After a ridiculously cold shower, he shaved, then dressed. Because it was November and he wasn't on assignment yet, he opted for a casual look: long-sleeved T-shirt, black jeans, and boots.

As he exited his small serviceable apartment near Parker, Colorado, he grabbed a jacket, then cast a regretful glance at the luggage that was stacked and tagged, ready to go to the airport. Good thing he'd purchased travel insurance.

A fifteen-minute drive brought him to the Hungry Bear Diner, one of Hawkeye's favorite hangouts. It was near headquarters, and massive, no-frills plates of food were served twenty-four hours a day. No matter when he walked in, Garrett could count on seeing some of his colleagues as well as local police officers.

Shirley Labelle had opened the place when she was first married, and the Colorado gem hadn't changed a bit in the forty-something years since. Modern buildings had sprung up all around the place, yet the diner stood as a testimony to the arduous work of the woman who still showed up and donned an apron every single day.

An overhead bell danced when he walked in the door. Shirley looked in his direction and shouted out a cheery good morning as she continued to cut a piece of her Mile High Lemon Meringue Pie.

Garrett bypassed the counter with its iconic swivel stools and strode toward the back of the restaurant, only to find Hawkeye already there, steaming cup of coffee nearby, and one waiting for Garrett.

They shook hands; then Garrett slid into the booth.

Before they could begin their conversation, Laura, his favorite server, walked over. She had one hand pressed to the small of her back as if to counterbalance her very pregnant stomach. "The usual, Mr. Young?"

Hawkeye answered for both of them. "We won't be staying."

There went breakfast. Garrett shrugged.

Without missing a beat, Hawkeye continued. "And the bill."

"Sure thing." Before leaving, she smiled at Garrett. "I meant to tell you how much we appreciated the gift card. It paid for a really nice crib. I'm trying get the thank-you notes written, but—"

"Not necessary. Just remember to name the baby after me."

"I keep telling you she's a girl." With a smile, she cradled her belly. "Rylie."

"Rylie Garrett." He picked up his coffee. "Sounds perfect together."

With a good-natured roll of her eyes, Laura promised to be right back.

Hawkeye set his cup down in such a precise way that it never clattered against the saucer. Then he leaned forward.

So much for pleasantries.

"Got a thirty-day assignment with your name on it."

"I was on my way to the airport when you messaged."

"Can't be helped." With zero concern on his features or even a hint of an apology, Hawkeye shrugged. "Headquarters will reschedule it for you and add another week to compensate for your flexibility."

Fair trade. "Where am I headed? Guessing it's not Mexico."

"Even better. Steamboat Springs."

The small, if renowned, resort town in the Rockies was about three hours away when traffic was optimal. "Isn't it a little early for skiing there?"

"The mountain opens tomorrow."

That had potential. The place was recognized for its light, fluffy snow known as champagne powder. If he could get in a few runs, life would be good. "When do I start?"

"Tonight."

He should have expected the answer.

"You'll be attending a fundraiser with a black-and-white theme. A tuxedo will be in your condo when you arrive."

Refusing the assignment had never been an option.

"The event is at a restaurant accessible only by gondola."

"Fancy." The enclosed type of ski lift was always Garrett's preferred way to make it to the top of a mountain.

"There are two stories. Bar downstairs. Dinner will be served banquet style. Afterward there will be a silent auction and a casino night on the second level. Band on the first floor."

A lot of space to cover. While it was still warm, Garrett took a drink of his coffee. "And my client?"

"Charlotte Connelly."

He sat back. The daughter and only child of Malcolm Connelly, no doubt.

Garrett knew of the man. His family had been members of the Zetas, a secret society, for several generations. If he recalled the story correctly, the original Connellys had started in the 1800s in the textile business and had acquired other manufacturing companies after the first industry suffered because of World War I.

Malcolm Connelly was as brilliant as his ancestors, and now his interests ranged from agriculture to manufacturing, electric vehicles, pharmaceuticals, even wind generation. If rumors could be believed, he was also involved with plenty of illicit endeavors.

Connelly and Company was also one of Hawkeye's biggest clients. Not only did they provide internet security, but they also protected the privately held corporation's physical assets and provided Malcom with personal protection.

"Where do I come in?"

"About a month ago, Aubrey Lewis, the primary agent assigned to Ms. Connelly got married and asked for a transfer to admin. Ms. Connelly declined to have another operative assigned."

His favorite kind of case. A protectee who didn't want him around.

"While she's in Denver, his protective agents watch her, so he doesn't worry as much. But she's headed to the family ranch for a month. She goes every year, represents the company at the event you're attending, then works remotely. Tries to get in a few hikes. Spends some time in nature. Dines out. Goes to the gym. Becomes another tourist."

And her father wouldn't like her being up there alone and so exposed. Garrett didn't blame the man. No doubt there were workers and caretakers, but still, for a woman who'd been a kidnap risk since she was born…?

Laura brought the check and a carafe of coffee that Hawkeye waved off but Garrett looked at longingly.

Hawkeye slid a fifty-dollar bill across the table. "Keep the change."

Wide-eyed, she glanced at Garrett.

Garrett grinned. "It will help with diapers…or something." Whatever babies needed.

Promising to see him again when she returned from parental leave, she thanked Hawkeye, then hurried off to help other customers.

"We've got two agents already on surveillance. And you'll have an entire team at your disposal. Also giving you Torin Carter and Mira Araceli."

"Heard they were a couple. Aren't they at Aiken?" He was referring to Hawkeye's Nevada training center.

"They will do rotations there. But we've found it advantageous to use them on assignment, posing as a married couple."

Which they would be soon if rumor could be believed.

"Jacob Walker will be an ongoing resource."

"Didn't he retire?"

For the first time this morning, Hawkeye cracked a grin. "So he said."

Garrett's phone dinged, the familiar tone of a message from headquarters, no doubt an encrypted file with a dossier and all the information he'd need, along with the logistical arrangements, including his cover story and where he'd be living.

"You're ops commander, and you have a two o'clock with your team at Walker's ranch."

"Aubrey Lewis available for a consult? I'd like to have her join the meeting remotely, if possible."

"I'll see what I can do. There's a jet at your disposal, and I'll have a driver at your place in"—Hawkeye checked his watch—"less than an hour." After rapping his knuckles on the table, he stood. "One more thing."

Isn't there always?

"Ms. Connelly cannot know who you are."

What the actual hell? "Jesus, Hawkeye. You want me to fucking lie to her?"

"Use whatever means you have to get close enough to her that you're inside her house."

BEFORE SEVEN-THIRTY A.M., GARRETT WAS JOGGING UP THE stairs that led to the private jet. He'd only been on a Hawkeye plane twice before. Military service had left him accustomed to uncomfortable, bare-bones flights, so he soaked up the luxury. The fact that Hawkeye had made the resource available spoke to the urgency of the mission.

As he stepped into the plane, a flight attendant smiled and reached for his carry-on. "Welcome aboard, Mr. Young. French roast is brewed. Cream, no sugar?"

This job was looking better by the minute. "Thank you. Yes."

"Garrett."

The voice, and the accent were as familiar as they were welcome and shocking. It couldn't be. He swung his head toward the cockpit. "Svetlana?"

"Good to see you."

He took in the former Russian spy, who was now Julien Bond's personal pilot. As always, she was crisp and professional in a tailored uniform, and a jaunty hat was perched atop her head. But none of that took away from the calculated gleam in her dark eyes. She could kill a man a hundred different ways, and torture him in a thousand more. And that was only part of her charm. "How'd I get so lucky?"

"I'm taking the *Tornado* home, so dropping you off is no hardship."

He glanced around. "So this is it?" The tricked-out, ultra-luxurious flying machine built by and for Bonds.

"As you said..." She tipped her head to the side as she studied him. Then she slowly gave one of her famous half-smiles. "You got lucky."

"How's married life treating you?" He glanced at her left hand. The diamond she'd been sporting the last time he'd seen her was missing.

"He's no longer...around."

What the hell did that mean?

"Make yourself comfortable, sir." The flight attendant jolted him back to reality. "We'll have you on the ground at the Yampa Valley Airport in about forty minutes."

"More *or less.*" Svetlana tipped her hat before returning to the cockpit.

His stomach took a nosedive. She'd flown fighter jets and was reputed to love exploring her current aircraft's capabilities.

He sat next to a window in a massive seat covered in butter-soft leather. The area around him was tricked out with wireless chargers and electronic gadgets. If he were braver, he'd look at the screen in front of him, showing the plane's telemetry. Instead he selected a channel that was showcasing a couple shopping for their own private island.

The flight attendant brought him a cup of coffee and handed him his duffel bag, and another attendant closed the cabin door.

He took a long sip of the strong brew, then quickly put the drink down as Svetlana began to taxi. Good God. It already felt as if she'd reached Mach one.

Since there was nothing else to do, he opened the file that headquarters had sent over.

Operation Snowfall.

Appropriate, especially given the upcoming weather forecast.

Because she refused protection and everything was secretive, the plan was more convoluted than normal, and it demanded a ridiculous amount of manpower. But Malcolm Connelly was willing to pay the price.

Two agents who'd been nearby arrived at the ranch less than thirty minutes after Charlotte had stepped foot on the property. In short order, they'd set up surveillance and deployed a drone. They had eyes on her. But not much more could be done until they had more resources on the ground.

He'd be staying at a two-bedroom ski-in, ski-out condominium. His cover was that of a cryptocurrency broker. And he was old army buddies with Jacob Walker.

His soon-to-be bride, Elissa, had donated a print to the evening's fundraiser, giving her and Jacob a reason to be there. He'd be going to show support for his friends. Torin and Mira would also be in attendance. They supposedly had several properties around the country and spent time wherever the weather was best. They were planning to buy near Steamboat and wanted to meet new people.

Though plans would be finalized later in the day at the Walker ranch, the recommended tactic was for them to watch the platform where the gondola loaded. When Connelly approached, they'd signal him to move, and he'd follow her into the car.

Which brought him back to his protectee.

The plane leveled out and headed over the freshly dusted peaks of the Rockies, and he entered the passcode to open the dossier. The more he knew about her, the better.

Pretty straightforward. Graduated top of her college class, currently single, one broken engagement, never married, and no known current romantic entanglement. In addition to running her father's holding company, she served as president of its philanthropic endeavors.

She was an only child whose mother died in a tragic ski accident when Charlotte was eleven. Since Malcolm had never remarried, she was the heir apparent to a corporation valued in the billions of dollars

The file had all the basic information, but it told nothing of the person she was. Spoiled or down to earth? Not that it mattered. Her personality had nothing to do with his job. He didn't have to like someone to save their ass. If that were a requirement, he would have stepped over the dead body of more than one protectee.

At the end of the information was a set of pictures, most of them recent and probably captured from the company's website. The largest showed her wearing a blazer, arms crossed. Had the uninspired business pose been her choice or the photographer's?

Her hair was pulled back from her face. She wore little makeup—a hint of nude lipstick, maybe a single swipe of mascara, nothing more.

But he noted her vitals. Blue eyes. Blonde hair. Slender build.

Absently he closed the file, then did an internet search. The first hit brought up an article on Scandalicious, an online gossip magazine. The first article made him raise an eyebrow: "Broken-Hearted Heiress." The accompanying picture was grainy, showing her getting into a sedan. If he was correct, the Hawkeye agent had been shielding her from the camera.

The article didn't have many details, but a representative for Connelly and Company confirmed that Charlotte's engagement had ended and requested privacy on her behalf.

A broken engagement was always shitty. When the news was fodder for paparazzi, it had to be worse.

Nothing could have prepared him for the next article.

It focused on her charitable works, and instead of the stuffy shot he expected, this was a candid, snapped on top of an unnamed mountain.

She was wearing tight-fitting, curve-loving black leggings and a puffy parka. Her blue eyes sparkled. A headband protected her ears, and her hair shimmered in the sunlight.

Her smile captivated him. It radiated freedom and pure, unadulterated joy.

"You're not what I expected, Ms. Connolly." He closed the file and tipped back his head. "Not what I expected at all."

CHAPTER ONE

HAWKEYE

Along with Torin and Mira, Garrett exited the SUV and headed toward Walker's house.

As he climbed the stairs, a roar echoed off to Garrett's left, and instinctively he reached for his sidearm.

"Stand down." Torin cautioned.

With a pounce, an enormous animal appeared on the porch in front of them. Then, hissing and spitting, it raised onto its haunches, standing between them and the entryway.

Mira laughed. "That's the welcoming committee."

In case it went for his jugular, he refused to take his eyes off the thing. "What the hell is it? A lynx?"

Mira's tone was light. "It's a Waffle."

"A what?"

"Walker's pet."

He lowered his hand. "Who the fuck guards their house with a mountain lion?" At least it offered lethal protection.

The front door opened, and a woman with dark wavy hair met them with a smile, a smile that faded when she looked at Garrett and the way he glared mistrustingly at the creature in front of him.

"Sorry." The woman hurried across the porch and sighed as she bent to pick up the wiggling, teeth-baring thing.

"Respect to you." She was braver than he was.

Tone somewhere between soothing and exasperated, she crooned in its ear. "We've talked about this a dozen times, Waffle."

As if a switch had been flipped, the hissing became a purr.

The change was so abrupt Garrett shook his head to clear it.

"I'm Elissa." The woman extended her hand. "You must be —"

"Terrified," he interrupted.

She grinned. "She has that effect on people."

"Garrett Young." Warily he accepted Elissa's hand.

"Waffle is a Maine Coon. She's a stray who thinks she owns the place. According to her vet, this kind of cat vocalizes more than others."

Vocalizes. Interesting choice of words.

Now that he was out of the line of fire, he appreciated her markings, along with the dollop of white on the end of her nose.

"Anyway, let's get you out of the cold before you freeze to death." Elissa entered the house, and he followed at a respectful distance.

When everyone was inside with the cold sealed out, he offered a better greeting. "Nice to meet the future wife of my old buddy."

She shook her head. "I'm not sure how we're going to pull off this mission of yours."

A few seconds later, Jacob joined the small entourage. "Welcome to Starlight Mountain Ranch."

"The views are spectacular." He'd enjoyed them more from the ground than he had from the airplane because Svetlana's airport approach had his stomach in knots.

"You should see it in summer."

Garrett shook hands with the operative he hadn't seen in years. He knew the man's reputation, heard of his heroics in Peru. Stuff of legends. "The peace doesn't drive you crazy?"

"It's helps keep me sane." He glanced at Elissa, and his expression softened.

Damn. Had he ever had that kind of reaction to a woman before? He tumbled through the inventory of his relationships and came up blank. Sure, he'd heard of love. But if that's what it looked like, he'd sure as hell never experienced it.

"We're setting up in the dining room. Three of our agents are already here. Waiting on Morrison. Two others are out on surveillance." Jacob pointed toward the rear of the house, and Garrett, Torin, and Mira headed that way.

When they arrived, the others in attendance stood to meet Garrett and said how much they were looking forward to working together.

Jacob had done an excellent job of transforming his home into a working environment, including enormous whiteboards and bulletin boards—complete with pictures of Charlotte and her home, even some aerial views. Blueprints were also tacked up alongside a map of Steamboat Springs. A large monitor was attached to the wall so that their protectee's former agent could join the meeting.

But that's where the resemblance to headquarters ended. Here there was an endless view of the meadow and a mountain beyond. And a sideboard held platters of cold cuts, breads, chips, even cookies.

The doorbell rang, and Waffle darted through the house. Garrett shook his head.

Less than three minutes later, everyone was onsite.

"The food is compliments of our new housekeeper," Elissa

said. "Soft drinks and bottled water are in the refrigerator. Help yourselves."

"Coffee?" Torin asked.

"There's a fresh pot in a carafe."

Things fell into a natural order. After grabbing food, Jacob took the chair at the head of the table with Elissa to his right and everyone else filling in.

As mission commander, Garrett stood. "Thanks for allowing us the use of your ranch, Walker."

"It was Hawkeye. Did I have a choice?"

People nodded or chuckled in sympathy.

Then Garrett addressed the operatives who would be providing surveillance. They'd received the same packets of intel he had. "As you know, we'll be covering the ranch twenty-four hours a day." This would be a hell of a lot easier if she were amenable to being protected. They could set up inside her house, and it wouldn't require this kind of manpower. Not that Hawkeye didn't know that. And Charlotte's dad was willing to foot the bill. "We'll use three teams of two people, eight-hour shifts. We'll rotate in new resources in one week unless you'd like to volunteer to stay on."

He waited for the team to nod. "You can either choose your partner or I can do it for you. Any volunteers for shifts? Or do we want to do it the old-fashioned way and flip a coin?"

Morrison spoke up. "I'm good for overnights."

"Same." A female agent nodded.

Quickly assignments were accepted, which left the team already on surveillance with day shift. "Good of you to leave the primo spot for the agents already in the field."

The two other agents would be on call to tail her and to fill in if necessary.

Headquarters had already provided descriptions of the

vehicles being used by Hawkeye employees. "Anything suspicious should be communicated. Anytime she leaves her property, we need to know. As usual, show up for your shift fifteen minutes early for a smooth handoff."

Morrison spoke up. "Got it."

"Tonight's event starts at seven. So we anticipate our target"—He paused to think. On radio communications, she wouldn't be referred to by name—"call sign Snow Queen, will be enroute up to an hour before that."

A member of the second shift acknowledged the order as did the agents who were going to follow her. "Copy."

"Torin, Mira, you'll be onsite with me."

"Outside in the cold." Mira affected a shiver.

If he were in Cozumel, he'd be drinking a rum punch right about now. His phone chimed, and he checked the message, then glanced at Jacob. "Agent Lewis is ready."

Within minutes, her image appeared on the screen. She was no-nonsense with short hair and a button-down blouse.

Garrett stood in front of the camera. "Thanks for joining us."

"This isn't going to be an easy job."

He waited.

"You already know she refused protection. And she's good at looking after herself. She can shoot competently and kick your ass if she's inclined."

He liked Ms. Connelly more and more.

"Charlotte's accustomed to looking over her shoulder, she's smart, and she doesn't trust easily. It takes time to build it."

Something they didn't have an abundance of. "What can you tell us about her habits?"

"She works out at the fitness center at the Chateau Sterling."

Right at the ski resort.

"Most often she'll get a coffee afterward at Java Nice Day. Sometimes she browses the shops and galleries downtown and has her coffee there."

Discomfort snaked up Garrett's spine, and he exchanged glances with Torin.

"Almost always she'll stop at the market before going home. And I'll tell you this. I've never seen anyone who works as hard as she does or sleeps so restlessly. She's awake half the night. Sometimes she bakes."

Interesting.

"In summer she'll hike. In winter she enjoys snowshoeing."

Covering that could be a nightmare.

"Occasionally she skis. Maybe once a week she'll have dinner with friends."

Every bit of intelligence was valuable. "Anything else?"

"She's a thoughtful person. She bought my wedding dress. Went all the way up the line at headquarters for approval since we're not allowed to accept gifts—kept asking until she got the answer she wanted. I'll tell you this: if she finds out what you're doing, there will be holy hell to pay." Agent Lewis walked a pen through her fingers. "Good luck. You'll need it." Then she ended the video call.

That was encouraging. "Questions?"

When there were none, Jacob distributed the electronics that had been sent to his house.

After everyone else left, he sat back down with Jacob and Elissa.

"Agent Aubrey is right. Charlotte is smart. I hate being part of something that tricks her."

"I agree that the situation is not ideal." He just hoped the whole thing didn't blow up in their faces.

IT WAS DAMN, FUCKING COLD AND ALREADY DARK AS GARRETT lurked in the shadows near the gondola building. Movies never showed how an agent's fingers turned blue and his toes froze in ridiculously thin socks stuffed inside a pair of dress shoes.

For the dozenth time, he slipped his finger beneath the bowtie at his throat. Since he could never remember how to knot the damn things, and Hawkeye hadn't provided one that clipped or just hooked together, he'd spent way too much time watching videos. He just hoped the results made him passable.

"Snow Queen acquired." Torin Carter's calm, measured voice slid through Garrett's earpiece.

About damn time. He'd been in the mountains less than half a day, and he was already tired of playing the abominable snowman. "Copy that." At a crisp pace, he headed inside the gondola terminal.

Mira spoke next. "I'm in place at the restaurant."

"Heading onto the platform."

"Roger." As he removed his earpiece and slid it into his jacket pocket, Garrett moved in behind Charlotte.

Her gown was full-length, and it hugged her rear as if she'd been poured into it. What part of this op had he thought would be easy?

There was no way she could possibly be warm with her bare arms, yet if she were uncomfortable, she didn't show it.

The lift operator greeted her, and she presented her invitation.

"Have a good evening, ma'am."

This lift was state-of-the-art, and she didn't have to step up to get inside. But still, there was a transition that he could use to his advantage.

He held out his own invite so there'd be no delay in boarding.

Snow Queen lifted the front of her dress. Holy *fuckballs*. The gown was slit to midthigh, and she was wearing stiletto pumps that whispered dirty things to his baser instincts.

Jesus. This was a job. Wanting to be close to her would never be an issue for him. Lying to her—about every single thing—might be. "Allow me."

She looked at him over her shoulder.

Her eyes radiated distrust. He wanted to sweep that away, slay her dragons. "I'd hate for your heel to get stuck." It wasn't a likelihood that it would wedge between the door and the platform, but it was a possibility in some alternate universe. "And another car is coming." Well, he'd read the specs. They had at least another thirty seconds, so he flashed a smile filled with charm as he offered his arm.

She glanced around before sliding her hand against his. It was warm and so much smaller than his, igniting his need to protect. Even if she weren't his assignment, he would have treated her the same way. "Always a pleasure to help. My mother would slap me into next week if I didn't treat a lady with respect."

Instead of reacting, Snow Queen moved to the far side and took a seat against the window, putting as much distance between them as possible. He winced. She was the first woman that line hadn't worked on.

He sat opposite her, allowing her the space she needed.

Seconds later, the door closed, and the cabin headed up Mt. Werner.

They effortlessly lifted into the air, traveling over hotels and homes, the lights beneath them like something out of painting.

Tonight's sky was inky, and the plump clouds moved slowly. For the ambiance he wanted to create, he'd prefer a more magical evening with twinkling stars and the moon peeping at them. Skiers and the resort itself would disagree with him completely.

Playing cool, he pulled out his phone and began taking pictures, then took a goofy selfie. Then, pretending to hesitate, he cleared his throat. "Do you mind? I'm terrible at this." He offered his phone to her.

For a moment, he thought she might refuse. But taking pictures of strangers wasn't an unusual request. Her not following social convention would be. "My sister doesn't believe I'm actually going to a fundraiser." He scoffed. Then he grinned. "Truth is, I wouldn't be if my friend's wife hadn't donated a picture tonight. He's an army buddy. Said it would mean a lot to them if I came." He extended his arm a little more. "You just have to touch that circle at the bottom of the screen."

Eventually she placed her tiny clutch next to her and accepted the device.

He spread his arm wide and made a ridiculous face.

Shaking her head, she brought the screen in front of her. As she moved, the wrap slid from her shoulders.

Her creamy, dreamy shoulders.

"There."

Exactly as he expected, her voice was firm and no-nonsense, just like the rest of her. Well, the damn dress was a surprise, and so were her shapely calves and legs that went on for days. And those fuck-me shoes…? There was more to the Snow Queen than anyone realized.

"I took two. Just in case."

Meaning he couldn't pretend the first one hadn't worked. Clever.

He pretended an interest in the pictures she'd taken, and outside snowflakes drifted past them.

The cabin slid to a stop and the doors opened. This time, the lift operator offered his assistance. Couldn't win them all.

Garrett slid his earpiece back into place and touched his mic. "Snow Queen's on the move."

Mira responded. "I'm in the bar."

"Carter?"

"In the car behind you."

Keeping a respectful distance, Garrett followed Snow Queen to the restaurant. None of his attempts at small talk had worked. He just hoped he'd cracked the ice enough that when they bumped into each other, she was a little more trusting.

While Charlotte mingled with a few friends, he headed to the bar. After securing a scotch, he stood with his back to a window, giving him a view of the foyer and coat check.

Because the upstairs was cordoned off for the time being, keeping track of her wasn't too difficult.

At the front of the room, the president of the organization announced that dinner was about to be served.

Charlotte joined the woman at table number one, and Garrett was sitting with Jacob and Elissa.

Champagne flowed, and that always helped to loosen wallets at a charity function.

After the plates had been cleared and dessert finished, the president thanked all the attendees and mentioned the donors by name. When Elissa's name was called, she stood and waved. Which meant Charlotte saw him next to her. Since the two were acquainted, he could hope it helped her trust him, just a little.

Then the president introduced Charlotte as the evening's major sponsor, including a twenty-five thousand dollar check to help young children explore their creative sides through outreach programs.

"Charlotte, do you mind saying a few words?"

With a regal bearing she walked the short distance to join the president and accepted the microphone.

"This is always one of my favorite events of the year, and it gives me a chance to get away to this beautiful place. Even the weather is cooperating to bring us a spectacular opening day tomorrow."

Over the past hour, the intensity of the snow had picked up, and it was blowing around.

"The arts have a special place in my heart. I've surrounded myself with pieces many of you have created. Sculptures, paintings, drawings, glass works. They all speak to me in a different way. Some bring peace or joy. Others are useful. And many are provocative, appealing to us on a soul level."

Interesting. Those were words he hadn't expected to hear.

"I'm sure you're anxious to open your wallets to bid on all the amazing things that have been donated."

Laughter rippled through the room.

"There's something for you specially, I promise. How about a vacation? Mexico? To wine country? We also have a few spa days available. Trips to the hot springs. Dinners at local restaurants. Or coffee for a year."

After each item, people cheered.

"We have something spectacular for you this evening. We've created a gallery-like experience onsite. At the back of the upstairs room you'll find a partitioned area. A curator has hung each piece and added lighting that will give you an idea of how the artwork will look in your home or office."

Interesting idea.

"We have art that will wow your senses. Imagine the thrill of owning a spectacular piece that's very likely one of a kind. Every bid you place helps support this community that we all love so much."

She paused, looking around. "We'll have plenty of entertainment tonight. A fantastic band. Upstairs, in addition to the silent auction items, there will be casino gambling. Craps, poker, roulette, and card tables. And with that…" Then her radiant smile lit the room. "Let the games begin!"

Yes, indeed. Let the games begin, Ms. Connelly.

CHAPTER TWO

HAWKEYE

Mira was sipping soda water in the bar area and had a clear view of the exit. And since Garrett guessed Charlotte would be staying at least long enough to greet the artists and mingle with her friends, he jogged up the staircase.

The roulette wheel had already gathered a crowd, and a woman shook the dice hard, then blew on them for luck before sending them to the far end of the craps table. More subdued players were seated in front of a blackjack dealer. Off to one side, a large group was gathering for Texas Hold'em. He saluted whoever suggested a casino night for a fundraiser. It seemed to suit this crowd perfectly.

He began to circle the room, adding his name to each of the papers attached to the donated items. Since it was early in the evening, he was certain not to be the top bidder, and it would help drive up donations. And if he did happen to win... Didn't matter. He was on an expense account, and Hawkeye would be the lucky recipient of something awesome. Well, except for the Kitchen Gadget Galore basket.

He sure as hell didn't know anyone who could benefit from that.

In his ear, Torin provided an update. "Snow Queen on her way to the second story. I'll follow so we keep eyes on her."

Garrett continued his rounds. If she happened to glance his way, he'd be preoccupied with whatever was in front of him.

After finishing up, he had two options. Either a little gambling or head to the gallery area.

That meant Charlotte would be out of view. But he could trust his team. Besides, her stumbling on him was better than the alternative. And if she saw him chatting with Elissa and Jacob, he might seem a little more approachable.

He caught Torin's gaze and inclined his head to indicate where he was going. Torin gave a surreptitious nod.

Elissa and Jacob were at the far end of the area, and he meandered in that direction. Clearly he didn't have the same understanding of art that Charlotte spoke of. A lot of it looked like splatters on a canvas. One, he supposed, was supposed to be dark and moody, and a woman stood in front of it, her thumb beneath her chin as she studied multiple angles. Hit him as depressing.

Another woman came into the small booth. "I will die unless I have this above my fireplace."

Seemed like an unfair trade.

The artist informed her that since she'd been by earlier, two other people had bid on it.

A connoisseur he was not.

By the time he reached the far end, a small crowd was gathered around Elissa. He offered a quick prayer to the paint gods that her work wasn't as uninspired as the others he'd seen.

When the piece came into view, he froze, stunned. *Holy fuck*. Why had no one warned him?

The portrait was of a naked woman spreadeagle on a bed, tied to the four posters. Her hair lay around her, a splash of red against the white sheets. Her back was arched, her mouth parted, and eyes wide with trust. It spoke of submissive surrender. It managed to be elegant and tasteful yet simultaneously erotic as hell.

He might not have an eye for talent, but he was willing to dive into his checkbook to own this thing.

Garrett rarely spent money. He didn't need to. He was often on an expense account, and his years in the military had taught him to get by on very little. Picking up and moving was a whole lot easier if everything fit into a trailer. This was the first time in his life he'd even considered purchasing anything in a frame.

And then, for a wild, wicked moment he imagined how Charlotte would look in such a pose. With a vicious shake of his head, he shoved the thought aside. She was clearly not a woman who'd yield to his dominance. Even if she were, she was a client. He had a job to do for another twenty-nine and a half days, then he'd be on a beach somewhere waiting for his next assignment and God knew where in the world it would be.

The couples in front of him moved on, leaving him alone with Jacob and Elissa.

"What do you think?" Jacob grinned.

"It's...stunning."

He glanced at his fiancée. "She's remarkable.

Elissa smiled. "You're loyal."

"But he's right." Garrett had a tough time keeping his eyes off the portrait. *Purity*, according to the attached gold plate.

And it was so captivating that he took the unusual step of adding his name to the bid sheet and increasing the amount by a full thousand dollars.

Charlotte neared, and Elissa's smile stiffened.

"We've got this." Jacob reassuringly touched her shoulder.

"How about an assist?" Despite her misgivings, he knew Elissa had remarkable composure. Months ago, she was the protectee of Jacob when a bad guy had broken into her workspace. She'd had enough presence of mind to take out the bad guy.

Drawing a breath, she nodded, then moved away from Jacob. "Charlotte!"

"She's good," Garrett acknowledged.

"She always comes through."

"So good to see you!" Though Elissa was gushing, it sounded completely authentic. "Thank you for inviting me to be here."

"I'm hearing that you're the star of the show."

The two embraced. Definitely a good sign.

"You remember my fiancé, Jacob?"

"Good to see you again." Charlotte's response contained a genuine note of warmth.

"Always a pleasure. Your speech was really good."

She shivered. "I'm not good at them. I'd rather hide from the limelight."

"Well, you're a natural."

Without missing a beat, Elissa continued. "And this is Jacob's friend from his army days, Garrett Young."

"Nice to formally meet you." He extended his hand, and she took it. Something powerful arced through the air. This close, he drank in her scent. Mountains in spring. Floral, refreshing. Damn intoxicating too.

"How did the picture turn out?"

"Picture?" Elissa glanced between the two of them.

"Ms. Connelly and I rode the gondola together." He used her last name on purpose, hoping she'd invite him to address her more informally. "She was kind enough to take a picture of me. My selfie game sucks."

A man who'd been drinking wine and lurking walked over to scrawl his signature on the bid sheet.

"Thank you!" Elissa called.

Garrett scowled. He hadn't expected his name to stay in the lead forever, but five minutes might have been nice.

When the lurker left, Charlotte shocked him by taking his place.

"Congratulations! No one else's offering has more bids than yours."

"Are you kidding me?" Elissa's eyes sparkled as if she couldn't believe it.

"You're ahead by thousands of dollars." And then Charlotte picked up the pen.

What the actual hell?

Was she doing it just to drive up the price?

Her hand froze, and she looked over her shoulder at him, her breaths in shallow, rapid bursts.

If the piece spoke to her the way it did to him, they had much more in common than he dared hope.

He swept his gaze over her, then returned his attention to Elissa. Even though he wasn't looking at Charlotte, he was aware of every one of her motions. "If I don't go home with this piece tonight"—which he fully intended to do—"I'd like to purchase something else." Now Charlotte would have no doubt that the painting also spoke to him.

"She has a website." Jacob extracted a business card from his wallet. "And she doesn't offer a friends or family discount."

"Jacob!" Elissa touched her arm.

"Your work is worth every penny. I wouldn't dream of asking you to cut your price." Garrett slid the business card into his pocket.

"A Genius is trying to reach you!" Loud music that sounded like a theme song from a movie erupted from Jacob's phone.

"Sorry." He grabbed the device with a shrug. "Julien Fucking Bonds. Always has to make an entrance."

"Bonds?" Charlotte echoed. "*The* Bonds?"

"Yeah."

"Our company runs his mainframe." Charlotte blinked. "And all of our computers are his."

And no wonder. They were solid and reliable, forward thinking, all while being exquisitely designed. If the outrageous tech genius wasn't already a trillionaire, he was on a trajectory to get there soon. His fingers were in every pie. Including the one Garrett wanted.

"He's a fan of Elissa's work. A collector. Greedy bastard." Jacob grinned. "Driving the price up for everyone." He checked the screen. "He'd like to place a bid."

Elissa frowned. "Is that allowed?"

"I have no idea." Charlotte furrowed her eyebrows as if in deep concentration. "Not sure why not. The rules don't prohibit it, and we are trying to make as much money as possible. I'll check with the president. In the meantime, hold off."

Jacob offered his phone to Elissa. "You want to be the one to tell him?"

"I"—she glanced around—"have people to talk to."

Shaking his head, Garret excused himself and said his goodbyes. "Nice to meet you again, Ms. Connelly."

He went downstairs to join Mira at the bar.

"Why are you here?"

"Hoping I'm not making a monumental mistake waiting for Snow Queen to come to me."

"This is a tricky assignment, Commander. I don't envy you."

Minutes dragged into an hour, and the snow outside turned into an actual storm with occasional gusts shaking the windows.

He and Mira passed the time eating peanuts and discussing operations at Aiken, along with Hawkeye's plans to expand the facility.

"It's exciting. What's not as thrilling is house hunting. We're hoping to be in a place we can call home by Christmas."

Home. That was a foreign concept to Garrett.

When he was a toddler, his mother decided being a military spouse—meaning she was often a single mom—was too much stress. When her husband returned from deployment, she packed up and left.

Fortunately Garrett had little memory of her, so the loss didn't sting as much as it might have.

Though his father tried, he was on an upward career trajectory and didn't have much time for him, which left him at daycare and with babysitters. They moved around a lot. As far as he remembered, his old man had never even owned a kitchen table. Not that he should judge. He didn't have one either.

"Snow Queen walking down the stairs."

Both he and Mira acknowledged the transmission.

Garret stood. "I'm going to head outside." As if he hadn't been cold enough earlier.

"I'll move closer to the exit."

They parted ways.

The wind was more brutal than he could imagine, gnawing on his ears. Cozumel seemed like a million miles away. But then again, he wouldn't be engaged in this cat-and-mouse with Charlotte. It was challenging as hell—and there was nothing he enjoyed more than that.

Mira spoke into his ear. "Snow Queen has her wrap. She'll be out the door in three, two, *one*. Hand off to you, Commander."

Garrett was comfortably seated in the gondola,

pretending to look at his phone when she stepped through the door.

When she saw him, her eyes widened. "It must seem like I'm following you."

He put down his phone. "If you are, consider me happily unconcerned." No doubt Mira or Torin stalled other people who might be leaving so when the cabin left the platform, they were the only two inside for the short ride back to the base.

She snuggled deeper into the wrap that was all but useless in this weather.

"Mother nature got serious, fast." He did what chivalry and Machiavelli demanded. He fished his earpiece from his jacket pocket, then crossed the short distance that separated them to drape it around her shoulders.

"Mr. Young, thank you, but I can't let you do this."

He returned to his own seat. "Blame my mother again. She'd slap—"

"You into next week," she finished for him. "She'd be very proud of you."

"I'll tell her you said so."

Despite her earlier protests, she clutched the lapels and drew them closer together. "Are you always such a gentleman?"

"I can be." He left his thought unfinished, hoping she'd fill in the blanks.

After a few moments where she seemed to consider his response, he spoke again. "The event appeared to go well."

"Better than we dared hope. I saw that you placed bids on everything. That was nice of you."

As if he were a nice guy, he shrugged.

"I'm still keyed up, to be honest. A lot of planning went into this. Kind of giddy. Like a high."

"Then you should let me buy you a drink to celebrate and unwind. You deserve it."

She clutched her tiny purse tighter, her knuckles turning white from the force of her grip. "I should...uhm..." Charlotte looked out the window. "Thank you, but I should probably head home before the roads get any worse."

"I hope you have four-wheel drive."

"Wouldn't be in Steamboat without it."

A gust of wind rocked them.

"Anywhere in the mountains, actually," she amended.

Once they exited at the gondola station, she started to remove his jacket.

"Keep it."

"I can't do that."

"I'd never sleep if I thought you were cold." He shrugged helplessly. "And, you know, my mom..."

She smiled.

"You really were fabulous tonight."

The next car arrived, and Torin and Mira debarked, moving into the shadows.

"Drive safe, Ms. Connelly." He gave a mock salute. Instead of heading toward the parking lot, he took the path that would lead to the Chateau Sterling. From the debrief with her former agent, it was the place Charlotte worked out and often grabbed a coffee. Which meant she liked it and was comfortable there.

He'd taken fewer than thirty steps and was questioning his strategy when her voice reached him. Garrett froze, then slowly turned to face her.

"On second thought I might enjoy a nightcap."

Mission accomplished.

He walked back to her and offered his arm as they left the building. The moment they were outside, snow smacked them in the face. Though the hotel staff was doing an admirable job of shoveling snow and spreading ice melt, it was a constant effort against the building storm.

Laughing, they pushed through the Chateau Sterling's revolving glass door, and he brushed a snowflake from her nose while she finger-combed her hair.

"That was crazy."

The hotel's interior was warm and welcoming, with dark woods and a massive stone fireplace in the middle. It was two-sided so that ambiance radiated everywhere. "How about there?" He pointed toward two chairs that were right in front of the crackling flames.

"Looks perfect."

Instead of sitting in a chair, she perched on the stone hearth, putting her as close to the heat as possible.

A server came over to take their order.

Garrett waited for Charlotte to go first.

"Champagne."

He nodded. "Make it two."

Mira took a seat near them, close enough to eavesdrop. And a quick glance confirmed that Torin was strolling through the lobby.

Their bubbly arrived quickly, and he toasted her. "To a successful night."

She exhaled. "I'm glad it's over. But at the same time, not. The planning is always fun, but I have a ton of nerves on the actual night. Will we raise as much money as last year? If we don't, which programs do we have to cut? And I want to expand, not pull back. All of them are important. And the fundraiser sets the budget for the entire year." She took a sip of her drink. "And next week, we allocate the funds. Then in January, we begin the process all over again."

"It's a lot."

Charlotte moved to the vacant chair next to him. Surprising him, she kicked off her shoes, then curled up on the cushion. "That's enough about me. I want to know more about you."

"Not much to tell." That would be the truth, at any rate.

"What do you do for a living? Besides rescue damsels in distress?"

This side of her, a little less guarded and more carefree, appealed to him. "That's my favorite thing."

"Seriously, though. I'm curious. Unless you're an independently wealthy man of mystery."

"Wish that were true. I'm a cryptocurrency broker."

"That's"—she tipped her head to the side—"interesting."

"Numbers. Calculations. Risk tolerance. Being able to read a crystal ball is a useful talent for the job." Then he moved back into more familiar ground. "It can be nerve-racking but preferable to being shot on a battlefield."

She shivered.

"Sorry. Shouldn't have mentioned it. Not when we're celebrating you."

"I'm grateful for people like you who are so brave. Making sure the rest of us can sleep easily at night."

"Not sure it was brave. For me it was a sense of duty. My father was military, and we moved around a lot."

"Is that one of the reasons your mom insisted on you having good manners?"

"Can you imagine if I embarrassed my father in front of his superiors?"

"Perish the thought."

"How about you, Charlotte Connelly, woman of the hour?"

She peered into her glass, seeming to watch the bubbles rise from the bottom.

Trying to decide how much to reveal?

"Nothing as dramatic as your life. My father is a businessman, and he expects me to take over the company one of these days."

Like him, she'd skirted the truth. Her father was far from a businessman. He was owner and CEO of a privately held, multinational corporation. She was not going to make this easy for him. "Is that something you want?"

"My heart lies in philanthropy, particularly the arts. As you saw tonight. But as you said, duty comes first, right?" Then, seemingly lost in the fire, she placed her glass on the hearth.

"Do you live far from here?"

She turned to look out the window. "Only a few miles. It's not bad when the roads are clear."

No doubt plows were either out or would be soon, along with trucks spreading gravel. Still, major roads were the priority, and the climb to the street leading to her ranch home probably wasn't on the top of the list.

"I'd like to tell you I'm fearless and that being on the roads when they're like this doesn't bother me in the least. But I've learned to appreciate only taking calculated risks. That caution kept me and my team alive."

"I can't imagine."

The condo he was staying at was close, but there was no way she'd agree to spend the night there.

Still, she made no real effort to move.

The server came to check on them.

"I think we're finished, thanks." Neither had done much more than take a small sip of their drinks. "I'll take the bill when you get a minute."

"I can pay for my own." Charlotte's objection was swift. And automatic?

"I'm sure you can. But my mother—"

"Would slap you into next week."

They grinned together.

"You wouldn't want that, would you?"

"In that case, thank you."

With a smile, the server moved off to help others.

For a few minutes, he and Charlotte enjoyed companionable silence. If this were an ordinary evening with an ordinary woman, he'd be content. Instead tension crawled through him. He'd been entrusted with her safety, and he meant what he said about duty. He took it very seriously.

Snow was piling up despite the fact it had been shoveled in the last few minutes. "I'm thinking of getting a room for the night."

"They've been sold out for months." She shrugged. "Opening day is tomorrow."

A group of at least six people pushed through the revolving door, spilling frigid air into the lobby.

Charlotte snuggled deeper into his jacket.

"In the interest of safety, I think you should stay with me."

"You'll never get a room."

"And if I do? With two beds."

She seemed to consider. "A suite."

Way to raise the stakes.

"With two bedrooms."

"I'll see what I can do."

"You'll never pull it off."

"I'll take that bet. How about a bottle of champagne to go with it?"

She requested a name brand and particular year that showed her exquisite taste.

"Your wish is my command." He stood. "I'll be back with the keys."

As Charlotte guessed, the clerk informed him there were no rooms available. So he asked for a manager and asked her to wait while he made a phone call.

When she agreed with a forced smile, he turned his back

and dialed Lifeguard at headquarters. The man considered miracles all in a day's work.

"Gonna need to give me a minute, ace."

This problem was likely going to go all the way to Rafe Sterling, owner of the hotel.

It took a few minutes longer than expected, but when Lifeguard called back, Garrett addressed the manager once more. "If you'd like to check your computer again, I think you'll find my reservation. Last name is Young"

"Sir—"

"Do it." He tipped his head to one side. "Please."

Same forced smile in place, she typed a few things on the keyboard. She glanced up, in shock, before she professionally schooled it away. "I apologize, Mr. Young. There may have been some confusion. I see you'll be staying in the Owner's Suite."

Well done, Lifeguard. "And we'd like a bottle of Dom. 2006."

"I'll have it sent up, sir." Instead of an electronic piece of plastic that resembled a credit card, she slid him actual keys. "Your elevator is over there." She pointed to a glass room with a concierge on duty. "If there's anything we can do to make your stay more enjoyable, please let us know."

"Thank you." He pocketed the keys, then turned back toward the fireplace.

What the fuck?

Charlotte was gone.

CHAPTER THREE

HAWKEYE

The next three days were beyond frustrating for Garrett. Had he ever had a more difficult assignment? A bad mood, lack of sleep, too damn much coffee, and an extra helping of impatience chewed on his last nerve.

Charlotte had spent all of Saturday at the ranch. With the weather, that wasn't unexpected. Sunday, she ventured out, but she just drove around then returned home. The Hawkeye team tracked her whereabouts, but Garrett had no opportunity to contact her.

Monday, she left her house before five a.m., then headed to the Chateau Sterling to work out. Hoping she followed the schedule Aubrey had provided, Garrett had gone to Java Nice Day, her favorite coffee shop in Gondola Square, opened his computer, and waited.

But she'd gone straight home.

Tuesday, her only stop was the supermarket, and she'd grabbed a to-go cup of coffee at the in-store kiosk.

Maybe he should pass his time there, squeezing fruit and sorting through vegetables.

Now it was Wednesday morning. The clock was ticking,

and he was no closer to getting inside her home than he had been last Friday night. Actually, with the way their evening ended, he was probably farther from the goal than ever.

He'd been up since four a.m., waiting for an update on her position. And he'd called Lifeguard and asked him to secure a workout pass at the Sterling for Mira. Maybe she'd have some luck getting close to their target.

At six, ready to snarl, he drove to her coffee shop, ordered a large cup of fresh brewed and settled in at a table that had a clear view of the door.

Today, Charlotte broke her pattern. At seven, she was still home. Eight a.m., same.

He tapped his microphone. "Anything?"

"Negative, Commander." Mira's competent voice reassured. "But I understand I'm embarking on an early-morning workout schedule beginning tomorrow."

"You're welcome. By all accounts, the fitness center is remarkable."

"I'll consider myself lucky."

"Is that sarcasm I hear in your tone, Araceli?"

"No, Commander. More like gratitude." But her mic was still hot when she laughed.

An hour later, he gave up and returned to his condo, where he'd spent too damn much time.

Shortly thereafter, he received a phone call from Aubrey Lewis, Charlotte's former protective agent.

"Just got off the phone with Charlotte Connelly. She wanted information on one Garrett Young, cryptocurrency broker."

That had to be promising.

"Told her I'd call her back as soon as I had a chance to do some research. Got your file open on my computer now."

"I appreciate the heads-up."

"Anytime." She was a professional and could be counted on to keep his cover.

An hour later, he received a text message from the surveillance agents.

Snow Queen on the move

Finally some action. He tapped out his response.

Is she headed to the Sterling?

She's turning that way.

Garrett grabbed his backpack and headed out.

"Back again?" the barista asked when he walked into the coffee shop.

"Couldn't concentrate at home."

He nodded as if he heard that story a lot. "Another large coffee?"

Why not? His hands were only shaking a little bit, and he wasn't sleeping anyway. "Thanks, yeah."

When he had his mug, he headed for his preferred table and seated his earpiece.

"Snow Queen is arriving at the Sterling."

Mira's words were the ones he'd wanted to hear.

He browsed the web, doing a deep dive on cryptocurrency so he could answer questions if she asked them.

A gentle snow began to fall, light and fluffy, the powder Steamboat was famous for.

"Leaving the Sterling."

He glanced up at the front door and waited for Mira's next update.

"Bypassing valet and heading for Gondola Square."

Hope sprang eternal. But hope wasn't a goddamn strategy.

"Headed for the coffee shop."

"Copy." He slid the earpiece into the pocket of his flannel shirt.

The overhead bell jingled when she walked in. Over the

laptop's screen, he watched her smash the snow from her boots. Damn if she didn't look sexy, even though she'd just come from the fitness center. She wore a black, puffy parka and leggings. Her hair was pulled back into a ponytail, and a headband protected her ears.

Without glancing his direction, she joined the queue and scrolled through her phone as she waited. He pretended to work. The truth was, she couldn't breathe without him noticing.

After placing her order, she moved to a vacant stool near the window. Then, when her name was called and she turned, she noticed him. For a moment she hesitated, then picked up her coffee and a bag, presumably containing a sandwich or pastry.

For a moment, she hesitated. Then she pivoted and headed for the door.

Damn it to hell.

Her hand was on the knob when she stopped and turned around, pulling back her shoulders as she made her way toward him.

Remaining cool and calm, he waited.

She stopped close to his table. "I was afraid you might have left town."

"Enjoying the mountain. Great conditions." The lies tripped easily off his tongue.

Her eyes widened. When she spoke, her voice held a wistful note. "You've been skiing?"

"When work doesn't call."

"You too? I've hardly been able to get outside."

"I'm hoping to get in a few more good days before heading out. Somewhere warm, maybe."

Shuffling her feet, she indicated a chair. "May I? I mean if I'm not interrupting."

"I apologize." He stood while she took her seat. "I should have invited you."

"I wouldn't blame you if you didn't."

He didn't take the bait. Instead, he waited for her to lead.

She stalled, pulling the lid off her cup to blow on the contents. "You travel a lot?"

"I get bored. Restless." That part was true. That's why the work at Hawkeye suited him so well.

"It's nice that you have that kind of flexibility." She took a sip. "Part of me wishes I did also."

"What is it that you do? I figured you were an executive."

"I hate that title."

"But is it true?"

"Yeah." With a grin, she replaced the lid on her cup. "My dad has a holding company."

One of the largest on the planet, though she gave no indication of that. "Is it public?"

"Private."

If he didn't have an idea of how to lead the conversation, he'd be completely in the dark.

"Anyway, I mostly help him."

"In other words, you're the CEO?"

"No. Thank goodness." She shuddered. "That's his position. Technically, anyway. He makes the strategy decisions, but I'm a member of the leadership team. Run the daily operations."

While he waited for her to go on, he watched her take a sip. Then she sighed with appreciation.

"The coffee here is the best in town."

"That's why I try to stop in." Before she could change the conversation—or escape entirely—he prompted her. "You were telling me about your important job."

"It's nothing like that." As he expected, she underplayed her role. "I'm a glorified administrator. We have a relatively small group—under two hundred people—and the department heads report to me. So I deal with HR, accounting, IT, that kind of thing. But just for the holding company. I don't deal with our subsidiaries."

"Call you Manager of Everything?"

"I like the sound of that." She laughed. "And maybe there's more truth to it than I'd care to admit. My heart is with our philanthropic endeavors. If I had my dream job, that would be it."

"But you get to work remotely. That's a plus."

"Actually I don't get that benefit. Most of the company gets to choose the environment that works the best for them. We request that our employees be able to be in the office with twenty-four hours' notice."

"Sounds reasonable, generous even."

"The leadership team has to go into the office at least three days a week. Dad feels it sets a good example and keeps us all connected. And there's the collaboration that happens when people are in the same space. Well, distraction as well."

"So are you on vacation right now?"

"This is my compromise. I live in Denver, but I insist on staying up here one month a year. Steamboat's only a few hours away from my home in Denver, as you know. And I can catch a quick flight if something is urgent."

"Why Steamboat?"

"There's something about the Yampa Valley area that feeds my soul. The views. The sense of community. It's so different than other ski towns."

"So." He leaned forward. She sucked in a breath, and for a moment he was so lost in the honesty in her eyes that he almost forgot his next words. "Have you thought about putting your foot down? Live here and spend time there?"

"Dad likes to have me nearby. And I enjoy it too."

"Understood."

"Well, you sound close to your mom."

Garrett chose his words carefully. "She's a special lady."

"I'm sorry. I'm keeping you from work." She pointed to his computer.

It was a newer Bonds model, sleek and fast as hell.

"Cryptocurrency investing, right?"

"I don't know about that. Could be considered closer to gambling, and with other people's money."

"I haven't bought any crypto yet. You think it's here to stay?"

"Nothing's certain."

"But?" she prompted.

"I'm not sorry I bought when I did."

"Maybe I should consider it."

"It's not for everyone. And you shouldn't take risks with money you can't afford to lose."

She grinned. "Isn't that what all financial advisors say?"

"At least the smart ones." Dodging lawsuits and absolving themselves of guilt if the markets went belly-up.

As he'd talked, she opened her bag and pulled out an enormous cookie, covered with thick pink frosting and sprinkles. Now she slid the treat to the middle of the table.

"I have enough to share. Help yourself."

Garrett rarely turned down desert, but this thing looked horrifying. That color of pink wasn't natural. Still, accepting her invitation would create a connection. He'd done worse things. Surely.

He broke off a piece and popped it in his mouth. He'd been right. It was cloyingly sweet. Thank God he still had some coffee left to wash it down.

A moment later she brushed the crumbs off her hands. "So…"

Setting down his mug, he waited.

"I wanted to talk to you…about the other night."

He sat back in his seat, giving her the space to make her way through the next few seconds.

Bravely she looked at him. "I didn't believe you'd actually be able to get the room."

"Sometimes you just need a magic touch."

"I'll be honest. When I saw the manager with the key, I freaked out a little. There are a million reasons why, but not one good excuse for ghosting you like that. I should have told you I was leaving."

"That would have saved me from worrying about you all night."

"You didn't…"

"I did." Well, most of the night anyway. Torin and Mira had followed her to the ranch, and then the surveillance team had taken over. Because of the conditions, drones had been inoperable, but that also meant any attempt to breach her property would be obvious. It had been a hell of a long night for third shift.

"I apologize for that also. You've been nothing but kind to me, and you didn't deserve to be treated that way."

Yeah, he did. That and so much more. "The hotel room was great." Or so he heard. When Torin and Mira arrived back at the resort, he gifted them the room. The champagne he kept for himself. He'd have shared it if Torin hadn't been an asshole and given him shit for losing his touch when she vanished.

At the postmortem on Monday at the Walker ranch, Mira had been his lone defender, saying Charlotte didn't trust easily. It was on all of them for not guessing she would run. Mira or Torin should have been in a vehicle, prepared for the possibility.

Remarkably she broke off another piece of the cookie. He'd need a big payment to take another bite. "While we're on the subject, I owe you an apology."

"You?" She put down the treat.

"I moved too fast, and I'm sorry."

"You were being chivalrous. And I know the room wasn't cheap."

No way he could have afforded it on his salary.

"You weren't asking for anything in return." She started to smile, but it fractured before it formed fully. "I tend to be a little wary of people. Life…"

Garrett waited for her to say more, but instead she shook her head.

To cover the awkward silence, he nodded. "Let's start over. I'll buy you dinner, anywhere you choose. I'll pick you up, and drop you off, like a proper gentleman."

"You won't try to kiss me goodnight?"

Fuck. His dick rose, pressing insistently against his jeans. He wasn't sure he'd be able to banish the image of her in his arms while he dug his fist into her hair and tugged it back as he held her fast, refusing to let her get away as he satisfied her, then sated his hunger for her. "I'll try to behave like a gentleman," he amended.

"I'd like to start over also. But I'm the one who owes you dinner."

He gave a mock frown. "You know my mom wouldn't be happy with that."

They both grinned—a glimpse of the intimacy he needed to build. For the first time, it didn't sit easily with him.

"How about if I cook? Would your mom be okay with that? And your male ego?"

"Really? You want to cook? Are you any good?"

"I understand I'm passable, and if you're asking if I plan to poison you, the answer is no."

He toasted her with his mug.

"Do you like Italian food?"

"My middle name is Luigi."

Sitting back, she regarded him. "Actually it's Christopher."

He raised his eyebrows. Was that information even in his file? Or had she gone deeper than Hawkeye knew? "Someone has been doing some research."

"Which is why I decided it's okay to invite you to my home."

Charlotte Connelly was a formidable opponent, as Aubrey had warned. He'd better never forget it.

Had she ever been more nervous?

With a frustrated sigh, Charlotte turned off her computer monitor. She wasn't getting any work done, so she might as well quit pretending. Refreshing her inbox wasn't productive.

What had possessed her to invite tall, dark, devastating Garrett Young into her home?

Yesterday, while sitting across from him, charmed by his wit and personality, it had seemed natural. But now that time was ticking, and she'd soon be alone with him and no distractions...

Her phone rang, and she grabbed it, wondering if it was Garrett. Before leaving the coffee shop, they'd exchanged contact information.

When she saw Bradley's name, she sighed. Not that she didn't like hearing from him. He'd been with Connelly and Company for fifteen years, and he was one of the most trusted members of the leadership team. He'd been instrumental in shaping their long-term strategy and moving them into some new areas—like artificial intelligence—while not sacrificing the operations that were foundational to their success.

Still, it was close to the end of the day. He wasn't Garrett, and she still needed to change clothes. "Bradley. What can I do for you?"

"How's your vacation?"

"I've logged over forty hours this week." And she still had Friday and the weekend to get through. The crick in her neck and the nagging headache told her how much time she spent in her home office. But like her dad, Bradley was old-fashioned. If you weren't in the office, it meant you weren't working.

"Malcolm has asked for another thirty-day period to review the acquisition of Workflow.ai."

"Seriously?" She sat back in her chair. The startup company was revolutionizing the ways teams worked together and helping to streamline processes. Everything she'd seen so far had been really impressive. She shared Bradley's opinion that it was best to close the deal now, before they became even more popular and the price went up. Or worse, the company was acquired by one of their competitors. "Why?"

"Concerns with how the rollout has gone at Connelly."

"Are they big ones?"

"No." Exasperation shot through the word. "Deploying software isn't an exact science. Glitches are to be expected."

Which they knew. Over the years, they'd dealt with lots of them. "What makes this different?"

"He doesn't seem like himself. I was hoping you had some insight."

"Seem like himself? In what way?"

"A little tired. He went home today around noon."

A note of accusation layered his voice. If she were there, she would know that. "I'll give him a call."

"This is a good acquisition, Char."

It was. And they'd been in the process for months. As far as she knew everything was on track.

On the other hand, her dad had not only held onto Connelly during all of the downturns, but they were experiencing record growth.

"You'll talk to him?"

"I'll keep you posted." Concerned, she dialed her father.

He answered on the first ring. "Charlotte. Good to know that you remember your dear old dad."

She laughed. They talked every day. "How are you?"

"Fine. Why do you ask?"

"I just got off the phone with Bradley."

"He's fretting about Workflow."

"And you." Which was by far her bigger concern, though so far, everything sounded fine in his voice. "You left early today."

Malcolm sighed with impatience. "Saw Dr. Van. And before you nag, just my yearly physical. Decided to work from home instead of going back."

"He said you looked tired."

"I was up late looking at Workflow."

"You want more time for due diligence?"

"Something I don't like in their list of investors."

Intrigued, she leaned forward. "Such as?"

"An LLC our team can't seem to find any details on."

Her dad had amazing instincts. If he thought something was off, it probably was. "Doesn't hurt to be cautious."

"How's progress coming on your part of the succession plan?"

She hated talking about this, even though she knew it was necessary. "We have years before this even matters."

"Proper planning…"

"Prevents piss-poor results." She'd heard his motto every day of her life. And he was right. Her grandfather hadn't done a great job of preparing for the future, and he'd died unexpectedly from a heart attack when he wasn't much older than her dad was now. The company had been in turmoil, and it had taken years to get it back on track.

Malcolm intended for everything to be clear, so that the transition was orderly when he passed. He wanted the right people in the correct leadership roles, and he needed to know where their weaknesses were so they could keep Connelly and Company viable for future generations.

But they had differences about how they saw the future. Of course she would continue to own the holding company. But she had no interest in being CEO. Because she was an only child, her father insisted on this...unless and until she chose to marry or have children of her own who could fulfill that role.

Which was something else she didn't want to think about for a long, long time. "I'll work on it." It was a half-lie.

Each week, all senior management turned in reports of how they'd spent their work week. Nothing too detailed, but it gave her father an idea of which projects were consuming the most resources. It also allowed him to see if certain things were being underrepresented. She'd log some hours on succession planning, so her father saw some progress. But she wouldn't give it a lot of her focus.

"I expect a preliminary plan to be finalized by the end of the year."

"That's a little more than a month from now." And they still had the holidays to get through.

He chuckled. "I have a calendar right in front of me."

"Dad, do you know how much work that is?"

"Considerable, yes. And I've been making the request for months."

Like others, she'd been dragging her feet. There were other, more pressing projects. "Who's the lead on this?" *Please don't say me.*

"Bradley."

She stifled a groan. That was even worse. But, maybe unlike her, he'd get the job done.

"I need you onboard, Charlotte."

Since he rarely made this kind of request, she gave in. "You can count on me."

"I knew you'd step up. It'll give us focus for the future, help us with long-term strategic planning."

It made sense, even if she didn't like it. "You promise you're okay?"

"Want to call Dr. Van yourself? But if you do, you have to send me your medical files when you go for your next... whatever they call it."

"Dad!"

"Next time Bradley calls you to tattle on what I'm doing, tell him to mind his own damn business."

She laughed. "At least he's got more work to occupy his time. He'll like that."

"Enjoy Steamboat."

"You should come up for a visit."

"I'll consider it."

Maybe that's where she got her ability to let fibs roll off her tongue. If her guess was right, he couldn't consider it for thirty seconds.

Finally she pushed back from the desk and exited her office, turning off the overhead light as she went.

The scent of lasagna bubbling in the oven wafted through the house. Earlier she'd also made a pan of tiramisu, and it was chilling in the refrigerator.

Her cleaning service had come over this morning while Charlotte had been at the fitness center. Then, despite a rigorous workout, she'd spent a ridiculous amount of time trying to burn off excess energy. In between phone calls, she'd walked through the house, plumped pillows, adjusted throw blankets that were fine where they were, restacked magazines, moved knickknacks, and checked and rechecked her watch. When she was in her office, her gaze continually drifted to the monitor that showed the security feed of the gate.

She'd been off her game all day, which was unusual for her, and she'd forgotten an online meeting until her executive assistant reached out to see where she was.

Now, as the minutes edged closer to Garrett's arrival, her nervous anticipation increased.

It had been months since her world collapsed in on her, shattering her heart. She'd sworn off relationships and especially love. Trust wasn't something she was prepared to offer.

Yet here she was, dashing upstairs to change for Garrett.

Standing in her closet, she scanned the racks and shelves, trying to decide what to wear. Nothing too revealing since she didn't want to send the wrong message. Which was... *What?* That she thought Garrett was kind? Polite? She sighed. *Sexy as hell.*

All of that and more.

She'd never met a man who appealed to her on so many levels. He was cloaked in mystery. Maybe from his days in the army? And that air was spiced by a layer of intrigue. He'd revealed plenty about himself but nothing too deep. Just enough to make her want more.

Aware of the clock ticking down the minutes until his arrival at six, she drew a steadying breath. *This isn't a date.* It was an apology for vanishing on him. Nothing more.

A renegade, feminine part of her brain whispered that she was lying to herself.

The truth was, she was interested in Garrett despite the millions of reasons she shouldn't be.

Even if she wanted a relationship, it wouldn't be with a man who picked up and changed locations whenever the mood struck him. Her life demanded stability. They were wrong for each other on so many levels.

So what was she doing? Inviting him out here was a waste of time and a huge mistake, one she shouldn't make.

Her hand trembling, she picked up the phone to call him and cancel.

CHAPTER FOUR

HAWKEYE

Suddenly a chime echoed through the room.

Charlotte closed her eyes. *Too late.* Garrett's voice—strong and forceful—drifted from a speaker. "Sorry I'm early. I was afraid I wouldn't be able to find your place."

Caught in a clutch of nerves, Charlotte crossed to the control panel on the wall. "That's totally fine." And it put an end to her agonizing. "Just give me a minute."

"I've got all the time in the world. And your favorite champagne."

Damn. He knew how to appeal to her.

She quickly dressed in casual slacks and a long-sleeved cashmere sweater. Then she slipped into a pair of heels. *This isn't a date.* If she told herself that enough, would she believe it?

After fluffing her hair, she went downstairs to the monitoring station in her office and pushed the button to release the gate.

He flashed a smile at the camera, and all her doubts disappeared, smothered by a jolt of anticipation.

Charlotte liked spending time with him, and just because

he was here didn't mean anything had to happen. Charlotte reminded herself he'd promised to behave like a gentleman. *Or at least try to.*

Part of her hoped he wouldn't keep his word.

Where had that wicked thought come from?

By the time his vehicle came into view, she had turned on all the outside lights and was lounging in the open doorway, hoping she looked casual, as if she'd just finished work for the day.

He opened his car door and stood. The breeze ruffled his dark hair, sweeping it back from his forehead.

At the coffee shop, he'd been wearing a flannel, but now he was in a long-sleeved T-shirt that showed off his powerfully built body. As if that wasn't bad enough, his black tactical pants hugged his rear in a way that should be illegal.

Her mouth watered.

He reached back inside before closing the door and walking toward her with purposeful intent. Her insides somersaulted.

When he reached the steps, he stopped. "Champagne?" He lifted the bottle.

Instantly she recognized the distinctive label. It was the kind of bubbly she'd requested the other night at the hotel. "You brought it with you?"

"No." He shook his head. "This is a new one. I drank the other. Needed to drown my sorrows. I hoped it would make up for the fact you weren't with me, but it didn't."

She winced.

Then he pointed to the bright bow. "Reminds me of your eyes."

Charlotte blinked. Her eyes were her most unremarkable feature. "They're ordinary blue."

"Maybe that's what your driver's license says." He shrugged. "But that's not what I see when I look at you. I see a depth of emotion and heart. I promise you, they're not ordinary."

Had she ever met anyone like him? "That's kind."

"It's a fact."

The evening air held a distinctive winter chill, and she stepped back, opening the door a little wider to invite him in.

Instead of walking past her, he stopped again. Even though she was standing inside, several inches higher than the porch, they were on eye level.

"Thanks for the invite."

"Thanks for accepting."

He leaned in. Close. *Closer.*

Her breaths turned shallow.

"May I?"

Every part of her hummed with awareness. Agreeing would be laden with danger. Yet she didn't want to deny herself of the experience. This was a one-time event, after all. "Yes."

His eyes wide, wide with intent, he leaned toward her. Then he brushed the lightest possible kiss across her lips, more whisper and promise than anything. It left her the slightest bit disappointed.

Garrett then entered the house, and she closed the door behind him, then turned the deadbolt, taking the short respite to gather her wits.

"It smells amazing in here."

From the kitchen, the oven buzzer screeched. "Through here."

She led the way to the left.

"Your place is spectacular."

"Thank you. It's taken years to get it this way."

"Inviting."

She loved that he saw it that way. "That's exactly the feeling I was hoping to evoke."

All of the wood—floors and beams—was a rich honey color, giving the place warmth. The great room had a massive fireplace with hand-selected stones for the surround. Couches and chairs were oversize and covered with buttery-soft leather. And local artisans had created the tapestries on the walls and the rugs that adorned every room.

In the kitchen, she instantly silenced the annoying alarm and grabbed a potholder.

"What would you like me to do with the bubbles?"

"There's an ice bucket in there." She pointed to a cupboard, then opened the oven and slid out the rack to gently ease the aluminum foil from the top of the pan so the cheese on top could get a little crisper. "Glass—with an etching."

He found the piece. "Is that a moose?"

"Isn't it wonderful? I bought it at a local gallery. The artist took a picture of one she saw locally and used it as the inspiration for the piece."

"It's unique. And of course, totally fits your style."

"Is that supposed to be a compliment?" She closed the oven and looked at him.

"Yeah." He nodded. "It is."

Effortlessly he moved around her kitchen and had the champagne chilling in less than two minutes. Then he looked until he found the glasses.

With her hips propped against the counter, she watched him and enjoyed sharing the space with him. Her father hadn't been up here for years and hadn't seen the changes. Everything was redesigned and new. The cabinets were deep blue, reminding her of a moody Colorado sky. As a contrast, and to soften them, she'd selected white stone for the countertops and the waterfall island.

He placed the glasses near the ice bucket. "I get why you wanted to stay home instead of going out for dinner."

"Honestly? I always hate to leave. Can I show you around?"

"I was hoping for a tour."

Charlotte intentionally avoided walking past him. If his little smile was any indication, he knew it.

The kitchen led into the sunroom. "This is my absolute favorite spot in the house." The floor was slate, and she'd filled the area with outdoorsy wicker furniture, couches, chairs, tables, and ottomans. "To make it cozy in fall and winter, we have additional space heaters. And of course, the gas fireplace. When my dad bought the place originally, there was a wall here, but I wanted to capitalize on the view without having to go outside." She looked at him, and he was studying her intently. "In the daylight, the view will take your breath away."

"I'd love to see that."

She hadn't meant it as an invitation, hadn't been intending to have anything together in the future. But maybe her heart was saying things her brain would warn her against…

Next they moved into the enormous great room.

"Do you spend a lot of time here?"

"No." It was too big for one person—empty, a little lonely. She hadn't turned on the television since the day it had been installed.

They ended the tour of the lower level in her office.

"This is where the magic happens?"

She exhaled and grinned. "I'm not sure I'd call it that. It's where I spend too much time on video conferences instead of strategic development."

When they returned to the kitchen, he looked around. "What can I do to help?"

"Right now it's under control. But thanks."

He pulled back a barstool that was propped beneath the island. "This really is the heart of your home, isn't it?"

"It is." For a lot of reasons. "One thing is that I can start something and finish it in the same day. Some of my work projects take week, months. Some of it is never done. And honestly, I think better while cooking or baking. It's as if my mind is free to concentrate on other things. And it feeds my creativity. The combination of tastes, colors, textures…" She looked at him. "I always wanted to be a painter, but I don't have the talent. So I guess this is my substitute."

"Or maybe you just didn't have time to pursue your passion?"

He was more insightful than any man she'd ever known. How did he do it? "That's one way to look at it, I suppose." She pulled the lasagna from the oven and placed it on a trivet to cool for a minute.

"I live on takeout and frozen dinners. So this is a treat."

"Then I'm doubly glad you came here." Except for the fact that the sight of him made her heart thump out a constant staccato. "Do you mind if we eat in the sunroom? I know it might be a little chilly." But it was less formal than the dining room, less intimate than sitting on the stool next to him at the island.

"As you said, you have heaters."

"Are you always so agreeable?"

He grinned. "The way to a man's heart…"

His smile was infectious. "Is through his stomach," she finished.

"Among the ways, yes."

There was no mistaking the innuendo, and her pulse skittered. "Uhm…" An image of him kissing her flitted through her mind, making her forget what she had been going to say.

Desperate to harness her wayward thoughts, she busied herself by grabbing the salad bowl from the refrigerator.

"There's a switch next to the gas fireplace in the sunroom. Do you mind turning it on?" Anything to get him out of the kitchen.

"Put me to work."

Once he'd done that, she handed him utensils, napkins, and placemats.

"I think I'll leave the food in here, and we can serve ourselves?"

"Good call. Not sure you could carry my plate with as much lasagna as I plan to put on it."

"What you don't eat tonight, you can take home for leftovers."

"Stop. I mean it."

Quizzically she met his gaze.

"You're gonna make me fall in love."

"In that case, it doesn't take much."

"I don't know about that." He shrugged. "It's never happened before."

Her mouth fell open a little. "Never?"

"Not once."

"So your heart has never been broken? Or you've never cheered getting away from the wrong person?"

He made a tiny X on his chest as if to indicate he was crossing his heart.

"That surprises me."

"Does it? Because I'm so irresistible? Or is it my good looks? Maybe the combination of all my attributes."

His *attributes* were definitely part of it. "All of the above."

"Ready for me to open the champagne?"

It was a pricey choice to go with this meal, but she wasn't about to object. "Please."

Minutes later they were seated around the table, and he raised his glass toward her. "Thank you for the meal. And for the chance to get to know you better."

Charlotte lifted her own drink. "To you. Thanks for the bubbly." She couldn't resist a quick, cheeky grin. "It's my favorite." And she'd cost him two bottles already this week. "But this it's a two-way street. I want to know more about you as well."

"Not half as interesting as you are."

After they each took a sip, he took an enormous bite of his food. He closed his eyes and moaned exaggeratedly. "Did I die and go to heaven? If so, I don't want to return to the land of the living."

His appreciation warmed her deep inside. The recipe was one of her favorites, and plenty of people had told her it was good. But not worthy of this kind of adoration.

Maybe that was him, though. She thought back to the way he'd gotten the room at the Sterling, and the fact he hadn't blinked about getting her favorite wine. The man didn't do anything by half measures.

"You mentioned it took years to get this place the way you wanted it?"

It was never easy talking about this. Maybe it was the warmth inside from the amazingly light champagne or maybe it was his company. He seemed genuinely interested in what she had to say. "My dad has always been a workaholic, and it was important to my mom that we had a place just for us to get away as a family, build memories. They planned to have a large family, and this would be a base, a place to gather. She wanted it to be big enough for extended family, especially my grandparents, a multigenerational experience."

"I can appreciate her sentiment. I think that kind of thing is important. Sometimes it seemed as if we were never in the same house for more than six months. I'm sure that couldn't have been true." He forked his last bite of lasagna.

"Another piece?"

"I'd rather hear your story."

Really? Most men she knew were more interested in listening to themselves or talking about mundane things: sports, or more likely, business.

"Mom was always frugal. Kept telling my dad the best way to save money was to not spend it."

He smiled. "Guessing that wasn't really a concern?"

"It was to her. She was a good steward of resources."

"Was?"

Grief was a constant companion, not as big as it was when she was younger, but still palpable.

"I'm sorry for your loss." Sincerity wove through his words.

She looked up and met his eyes, reading compassion in the rich, green depths. "It was a long time ago."

"Still…" With incredible gentleness that she would have never guessed him to be capable of, he touched her hand.

"Thank you. Because this place meant so much to her, I always feel a little closer to her when I'm here." She took a drink, mostly as an excuse to pull away her hand so she didn't do anything reckless, like deepen the intimacy.

"How did your family end up buying this place if she wanted to save money?" He scooted back a little and propped his ankle on his opposite knee, as if he had all the time in the world to listen to her.

"Dad wanted to be within driving distance of Denver, of course."

"Makes sense."

"And needed an airport nearby. But Mom wanted a bargain. Vail and Aspen and a lot of other places along the I-70 corridor were not cost-effective. Price per square foot was ridiculous."

"Sounds shrewd."

"She had a very strong personality."

"I'd say she passed it along to her daughter."

With a good-natured laugh, she wadded her napkin and tossed it at him. "Anyway, she narrowed in on Steamboat and found a great agent. Gave him the checklist and a budget that was about half of the going rate."

"Half?"

"And said not to call her until he found something. She was able to wait." She traced a random design on the base of her glass. "It took about six months, but he found a seller who was in financial distress. He needed to unload the property and was willing to sell for little more than he still owed on the mortgage."

"I'm impressed."

"Mom said it had good bones, and it definitely does." Despite the fireplace, the evening chill was creeping in around them, and she turned on another space heater. "We came up here as often as we could, every Thanksgiving, every Christmas. And me and Mom would stay here over the winter holidays, and Dad would fly back and forth. It was a perfect place to be. Skiing, ice skating, snowmobiling, snowshoeing."

He finished his champagne, but held onto the glass.

"I never wanted to leave."

"I understand the sentiment."

"Then Mom died. One of those horrible, freak things. We were up here for spring break, and we were having a family outing on the mountain. I had a private ski instructor for the first half of the day. Then we were going for lunch and spend the rest of the day together."

With the infinite patience she was coming to expect and appreciate from him, he silently waited, giving her the space to unravel the story at her own pace.

"Mom and Dad were on an advanced run, and it was spring conditions, meaning it was icy. As I understood it,

Dad skied ahead, and she stopped to take a picture of him. Long, awful story short, she was hit by an out-of-control skier. A complete accident. If she hadn't taken her helmet off when she stopped, if there'd been fresh snow, if that rock hadn't been exposed... Dad saw it all, and he was powerless to save her. Can you imagine watching something like that?"

"That would fuck up the best of us."

"I was eleven. It changed everything for us. Dad tried. He knew how much the ranch meant to me, so he got a nanny, and we came for Christmas. But then work called, and no one could tell him no, so we went home." She lifted one shoulder. "I honestly think the memories here were too strong for him to deal with. He even sold the house we were living in at the time. Started completely over. That's to be expected, I guess."

"That compounded the loss for you, didn't it? Not only was your mom gone, but the future she wanted to create. You moved, and you no longer had the ranch to escape to."

"At least he didn't sell it. As soon as I was old enough, I started coming up here by myself. Then I began molding it to my vision a few years ago."

"Has your dad seen it?"

"No. I keep inviting him. But his responses are always vague." At some point, she had to accept the fact that he probably never would.

"Did he remarry?"

"No. Mom was the love of his life." She looked at him, saw the compassion on his face. "He said he never wants to experience that level of heartache ever again."

"Are the two of you close?"

"Very. We talk at least once a day, and I see him for dinner on Wednesdays. We occasionally do something together on the weekends. Of course I'm his hostess for events."

"You enjoy it?"

"I do. But he's overprotective. He doesn't think I know, but that's part of the reason he still wants me to come into the office. We have a security team, and if I'm there, he can keep an eye on me."

"Has he always been that way?"

"He didn't even want me to go away to college. So I stayed in Denver. A few years ago, his best friend's daughter was kidnapped."

"Overseas?"

She finished her drink. "You might expect that, but no. Here in Colorado. The family did as the kidnappers wanted. They kept out of the press, and they didn't involve law enforcement. But Dad was there with them, at the house, every minute for three days. He saw everything, all the anguish, the fear."

"That scared him. I don't blame him."

"I think it's why he panicked. He hired a bodyguard for me, installed an alarm and a panic button up here as well as at my house." She exhaled. "He threatened to sell the ranch if I didn't bring Aubrey with me."

"Where is she now?"

"She got married and wanted to be home more. So I took the opportunity to put my foot down. To say he's not happy with that decision is an understatement."

"You're his only kid, right?"

"Yeah. After he lost Mom, he swore he'd never let anything happen to me."

"Can you blame him?"

"Garrett, seriously…"

He dropped his foot to the floor and leaned forward.

"He showed up at my senior prom."

Garrett laughed.

"You know, I hope that one day he finds love again. He's far too young to spend the rest of his life alone."

"What about you? Do you want to fall in love? Get married?"

The question, no matter how conversational, was a knife in her heart. She'd wanted love and happiness, just like all of her friends. Then she discovered that she never measured up for Andy, no matter how hard she tried. Not in life. Not in bed. "You know, it's really cold in here." It was, but until right then, it hadn't bothered her. She gave a practiced half smile before standing to gather her plate.

"Sorry. I didn't mean to strike a nerve."

"You didn't."

He remained where he was, thoughtful, head angled to one side. His eyes darkened, and she knew he saw through her lie. "Would you like me to go home? Or would you like me to stay?"

CHAPTER FIVE

HAWKEYE

Garrett regarded her, waiting for her answer, but doing nothing to influence her decision.

She struggled for honesty. "The truth is, you're right. It is a tender spot. I almost got married a few months ago." The pain and humiliation were still fresh. "It didn't work out."

"Whatever happened, he clearly didn't deserve you. And you sure as hell don't deserve to feel like shit because he was an ass."

"How do you know it wasn't me who was the ass?"

"Because you wanted the happily ever after. You wouldn't have fucked it up."

"Did you just look in that crystal ball of yours again, the one you mentioned the first night we met?"

"As I said, it's a handy skill to have." He smiled.

The fact he'd realized he'd said something wrong and immediately apologized meant something to her. Especially after all of Andy's excuses and lies, then twisting things around in an attempt to make her look bad. "We still have champagne."

A slow, inviting smile curved his lips. "Does that mean I'm staying a little longer?"

"Yes. If you help with the cleanup."

"My mother—"

She laughed. "Would slap you into the next week if you just went and sat on your butt while I did the dishes after preparing the meal?"

"It's as if you know her."

His ridiculousness dissipated the reminder that no matter how hard she'd tried, she had never been enough for Andy, either in life or in bed. "I happen to agree with her on this one."

She pointed out where the foil and plastic wrap were to cover the lasagna and salad while she started to rinse their plates to put them in the dishwasher. Fortunately she'd cleaned up after herself as she'd prepared the meal, so there was very little work remaining.

"What's this?"

She glanced over her shoulder to see him standing in front of the open refrigerator. "Oh. That."

"Charlotte…" A growling, sexy note cut through his voice, shooting ripples of awareness through her.

"Dessert."

"It looks like tiramisu." He grinned like a fool.

"It is."

"That's it. Set the wedding date."

His enthusiasm was pure and infectious. "Slow down, cowboy. What do you bring to the union?"

"That's a tough one." He closed the refrigerator.

After she dropped the silverware into the basket, she closed the dishwasher, then dried her hands.

He was still near the refrigerator, tapping his finger on his chin. "I know! I can uncork champagne for you."

"That does come in handy."

"In fact, I have a wide range of skills. I can get into beer and wine bottles with ease. That's handy, right?"

"Absolutely. We'll add that to the list."

"Speaking of…can I refill your glass?"

"That would be nice. Thanks."

"And turn off the heaters in the sunroom?"

She'd forgotten.

"Or would you like to go back out there?"

"I thought maybe in the great room." With him here, the space suddenly seemed more inviting.

Minutes later he'd turned on the lamps and flipped the switch to light the fireplace, and they were seated on opposite ends of the couch.

Because the furniture was so large, she kicked off her shoes and curled into the corner.

"This thing you do with your shoes…kicking them off, having them land one on top of the other…"

She studied him over the rim of her glass.

"You did it at the hotel too."

It had been so long since she'd been romanced that she had no idea what was happening here. *Flirtation?* "Foot fetish, Mr. Young?"

"Is that the same as a shoe fascination?"

Her hand trembled, so she put down her drink. "I have no idea."

"Me either." He focused his gaze and all of its intensity on her. "But I do know I will be thinking about those shoes before I fall asleep tonight."

No doubt her mind would replay this moment: the dancing flames; the deep, rich timbre of his voice; and the way his green eyes had darkened.

"It makes me think…"

Curious, she waited for him to go on. One thing she already knew: she had no idea what he would say next.

"About Elissa's portrait. The one she donated to the fundraiser."

His words electrified her. Their conversation had taken a turn, and now it bordered on dangerous territory.

"The painting spoke to me."

"Did it?" She feigned disinterest, but her voice was a higher pitch than it had been a moment ago. Common sense urged her to shut down the conversation. But there was something much, much bigger at play. "In what way?"

"Purity."

"The title definitely fit." Though Charlotte might not be an artist like she wanted, she recognized the depth and emotion imbued in the work.

"The model looked pure, no pretense. Open. Trusting as if she knew she were in safe hands."

On some dizzying, disorienting level, Charlotte knew they were having a different conversation. This wasn't about the model. It was about her, and he was offering his reassurances. Whatever she wanted was okay with him.

For her, trust would take time, if she was ever capable of offering it again.

"Who won the auction?"

He'd seamlessly changed the subject, allowing her to breathe and hopefully drag her heart rate back under control. "Julien Bonds."

"Of course he did. He tends to get whatever he wants. I'm surprised he was allowed to bid."

"The president considered the situation and had a quick meeting of the executive board. In a way it didn't seem fair. But the point of the entire evening was to raise funds. So they told him that he had to find a proxy."

"Guessing that wasn't a problem?"

"From what I understand, there was a line of women, and a few men, crowding each other out. Who wouldn't want to spend a couple of hours on the phone with him? A direct line to a gazillionaire?"

"How did they decide?"

"It was a fundraiser, right?"

"You had people bid for the honor?"

"It was a frenzy."

"Brilliant. Who won?"

"Phyllis Newton. She's a widow with millions to spend and a crush on Julien." She leaned forward to grab her drink, but he was faster, picking it up and offering it to her. "I think she developed writer's cramp. Every time someone put down the pen, she picked it up again. I guess it was a spectacle. They ended up moving out the partitions to accommodate the crowd."

"They're calling the fundraiser a success?"

"Beyond our wildest expectations. He sent out a press release the next morning, mentioning Elissa by name. He said he now has eleven of her originals in his collection."

"Impressive."

"And he mentioned our fundraiser and talked about the amount of good that we do for the community."

"Well, by extension, the good he does."

She shook her head. "Are you always such a skeptic?"

"I've found no one is all good or all bad. Humans are complex. And you can never really know anyone."

His answer was more profound than she expected. Did it also offer insight into him personally?

"But it also means the picture is not going to be hanging in your house or mine."

Charlotte's heart flipped over in her chest. She debated how to handle this. Confess she'd wanted it? Or pretend she'd been just trying to do good for the community? "Like you, I placed a lot of bids that night." Damn it. The small fib made her shift uncomfortably.

Fingers steepled together, he regarded her.

Does he see the truth?

"I wanted it."

His admission—so unexpected—took her aback. "You did?"

"How about you?"

"I…" She blew out a tiny breath. "I wanted it too, for all the reasons you said." Dare she be brave? "It spoke to me too."

"What appealed to you?"

"The model's anticipation. She's confident in her surrender, and she knows he will give her what she wants."

Once again the atmosphere was heavy with subtext. He'd given her a way to talk about things that weren't discussed in polite circles, to test the waters between them. *Oh God*. She craved his touch despite a million reasons she shouldn't. But the force of her desire—so real it was an undeniable hunger—plowed into her.

"And what is it that she wants?"

She looked at the empty spot above the fireplace where she would have hung the artwork. Severing their gazes allowed her to admit to things she might not have. "Peace."

Even though she didn't turn her head, she was aware of his intense scrutiny. "Tell me more about that." It wasn't just a question; it was an invitation.

Then she did look at him because she wanted him to understand. "There are times, places, where stress"—*and the world's demands*—"can't reach you. Where you can disappear and forget everything."

"Is that what BDSM is for you?"

Her breath caught, then froze in her throat, a massive knot of anxiety.

Again, as if he had all the time in the world and nowhere else he'd rather be, he waited.

"I don't talk about this."

"Not ever? Or not now?"

Except for the gentle hum of the heater, the house was silent, and nothing existed in the world except for the two of them. "The whole thing is complicated."

"I do complicated well."

Charlotte believed him. It wasn't just the military service; navigating the volatile cryptocurrency market couldn't be easy either. "It's not about the pain necessarily. It's about the release. Endorphins. It takes a lot for me to unwind."

With care she selected her words, attempting to put her internal world into some sort of context that made sense. "I don't have a huge amount of experience. But a couple of times, I was really able to let go, to a place where I had no problems. And when it was over, I was relaxed but on a deeper level."

"The peace you spoke of."

"Take me there."

"Fuck. Charlotte…I don't…we don't…"

"Yes. It doesn't have to mean anything." In fact, she couldn't allow it to. This was nothing more than something they both wanted.

"It may not mean anything to you, but I can't promise it won't to me."

She shook her head. "No strings."

"Woman, you don't ask for simple things."

"Just some time together. And we both go our separate ways."

"I can't do that."

Exasperated, beyond frustrated, she sighed. He might be the only man on the planet who would refuse her request.

"BDSM requires negotiation. I'm willing to take you wherever you want. In fact, it would be my honor."

An image of her over his knee teased her.

"But I won't pretend this means nothing to me. You're

offering a piece of yourself to me, and I'm offering the same in return. I won't spank you and leave you. I'll be with you until you're back both mentally and physically, no matter how long that takes."

"I—"

"Take it or leave it."

The earlier, approachable, joking man was gone, buried beneath a tough dominant shell. She hated it as much as she respected it. "I don't even know what that means."

"So tell me more about your experiences."

"There's a club in Denver."

"The Reserve?"

She nodded.

"I'm a member."

The information provided an extra layer of reassurance for her. "I've only been there as a guest." Members had to pass a stringent background check, and the initiation fee was outrageous.

"What part did you like?"

"I scened a few times with a Top. Master Devon."

Garrett nodded. "I know him."

"I was on a spanking bench." The whole thing was surreal but in a wonderful way. Master Devon didn't have a relationship—and he kept it that way. He taught classes, gave demonstrations, and each Saturday night he attended the club where he fulfilled the desires of unattached submissives. "And I was curious. He's really tuned in to his bottom's hopes. Made me talk about it before having me get into position." She wiggled around to look at Garrett more closely. "You remind me of him."

"I'm pleased. He's respected in the community."

Charlotte narrowed her eyes, hoping she had the magic words to get him to agree to her terms. "He has no expectations."

"Then that's where we part ways. I don't allow my submissives to walk away and potentially experience an emotional upheaval afterward."

My submissives.

Her nerves plunged to the bottom of her stomach. "I thought you didn't have relationships."

"I don't. But I'm not an asshole."

"Master Devon is not—"

"I didn't say he was. Aftercare is important to me."

She scowled.

"Do you agree to my terms? Or would you prefer to go to bed tonight to toss and turn? Or do you want a taste of what could be?"

"A taste?"

"We've both had a glass of champagne."

And plenty of food and at least two hours had passed.

"So there can't be anything too serious." He turned to her and slowly reached his hand toward her, capturing a lock of hair and twining it around his finger. "What will be? We can get together tomorrow instead if you'd rather. Or we can have a teaser this evening and agree to a longer scene at a later date if you find the experience agreeable."

His voice, with its soothing cadence, hypnotized her. "I want this. Tonight."

A slow, satisfied smile toyed with his lips. "And a safe word?"

"Steamboat."

"Makes sense. And to slow down?"

She usually went with yellow, but a different answer came to her. "Blue."

"That's an interesting choice."

"Not really. It's the color for an intermediate ski run."

"Ah. In keeping with a theme. Green for easy, beginner. Black for difficult, advanced."

"Exactly."

"Blue it is." He withdrew his finger, leaving a corkscrew curl next to her cheek.

Then he moved closer to her so that he was sitting almost in the middle of the couch. He looked so at ease, so damn controlled and dominant, that every submissive instinct sparked to light as if a fire had been lit inside her.

"I want you to take a moment to ensure that you know what you're doing and that you won't have regrets."

Charlotte had never been more certain of anything.

"When you're ready, strip down to your bra and panties."

His voice was different than it had been earlier, deeper, commanding, rather than questioning.

He couldn't know how difficult the request was. Because of her workouts, Andy had sneered at her for being too athletic looking. He preferred women who were a little softer. Which in the end, he'd gotten. "I always wear workout gear at the club."

"We're not at the Reserve."

And he definitely wasn't the disinterested Master Devon.

She took hold of her sweater and drew it up and off, allowing it to splash across the arm of the couch.

Garrett's eyes flared with approval, emboldening her.

Then she stood to remove her pants. Those she allowed to fall to the floor, then left in a puddle and walked to him.

"You're sensational, Charlotte."

She drank in his approval, then accepted the hand he offered.

"I'd like you to lie facedown across my lap, keeping your body on the cushions for support."

This wasn't what she expected, and getting into position felt awkward, but he was there with his strong hands on her body, guiding her into position.

"That's it."

"Comfortable?"

She turned her head to the side. The question was somewhat ludicrous. "As much as possible." His tactical pants were rough beneath her bare belly, and the leather cushions were warm.

Slowly he trailed his fingertips beneath her buttocks. Then he traced the outline of her panties.

"There'll be nothing that's too hard. I'll be paying attention to your breathing, your reactions. There's no need to clench. Just offer yourself up for each spank when you're ready."

She nodded.

"I need your words, Charlotte. Your agreement. Your understanding."

"Yes, Garrett."

He continued his lazy exploration, stroking the insides of her thighs. "I will not be touching you intimately. This is about the impact only."

Just like she was accustomed to.

He squeezed her ass cheeks, kneading them, releasing them, and her flesh quivered.

"I'm waiting."

"For?"

"You to raise your hips, your body begging me to give you what you want." He danced the lightest of touches down her spine.

Though her nerves were ragged, he soothed her.

She took a breath then wiggled a little, raising her buttocks.

The spank was barely there, a whisper.

And he didn't offer another until she silently asked for it.

It took a dozen, maybe more, swats for her to find a rhythm, then for her to position her hips so that she was always ready to accept his offering.

Once she was relaxed, she turned her head to the side, staring at the fire, mesmerized by the ever-changing flames.

She sighed softly as they seemed bigger, closer. Then she closed her eyes.

"Are you doing okay?"

In response, she gave a deep sigh.

"Charlotte?"

"Mmm."

"That's a yes?"

Go away. "Yes."

Over the next few minutes, he increased the tempo and, ever so slightly, the force, and it was enough to send her deep. Deeper. A place where the flames now flickered inside her mind, and she was one with them. Fear, worry, doubt was swallowed by the rhythmic fall of his cupped palm spanking, caressing the flesh she offered to him.

"Charlotte?"

This was magical, and she couldn't stop smiling. Though she'd been able to let go at the club, it was nothing like this. The quiet of her own home, and the ministrations of a man who was focused solely on her.

"Time to come back."

"Hmm?" On some level, she became aware that the spanking had stopped.

Gently he drew her to him, turning her body as he did so.

She scowled, never wanting it to end.

But he was bigger, stronger, and much more determined. He helped her to sit up but kept her cradled against him. Then he wrapped her in a blanket.

He kissed the top of her head, and that brought reality back.

Disoriented, she blinked her eyes open.

She'd been aware—peripherally—of being moved and not

wanting to. But she was in Garrett's lap, cradled in his strong arms.

"How are you doing?"

Before answering, she took inventory. She was relaxed. Her rear was a little tender, and her body was dewy with perspiration. "I'm okay. I think."

"You were gone for a while."

"How long?"

"Twenty minutes. Maybe a little longer."

"That's not possible." She would have guessed five at most.

For a woman who insisted she didn't want aftercare, she was completely content to remain snuggled against his chest, soothed by his strong heartbeat beneath her ear.

She reevaluated his earlier question and realized she was relaxed on a level she hadn't been in years. "Thank you."

"My pleasure entirely." He took her chin to tip back her head. Then he brushed another gentle kiss across her lips.

As if it were inevitable, she opened her mouth to him, and he accepted the invitation, kissing her deeply, claiming her. She curled her arm around his neck, wanting the moment to last forever.

The taste of him, the sweetness of champagne, was sexy, making her want more. She touched her tongue to his, and he moaned, taking more, demanding.

Then, with a groan, he pulled back. "I don't want to mix up your spanking with sex."

"It was only a kiss."

"No." He shook his head. "It was a prelude, and we both know it."

He was right. It would be easy, natural to straddle him or ask him to take her upstairs.

"That's not what we agreed to."

"Are you always so noble?"

He scoffed. "Don't confuse me with a hero, Charlotte."

Another few minutes passed before she was ready to move from his lap.

When she stood, he kept his hands on her waist until her footing was sure.

"You may feel that spanking a little bit in the morning."

"I hope so." She scooped up her sweater and pulled it back on. Then she slipped back into her slacks.

"Your Dominant prescribes a hot bath and some arnica if you have it."

Your Dominant.

That thought sent possibility spiraling through her, and she quickly tamped it down. There was no possibility of him being that, at least in a long-term role. She was in Steamboat temporarily, and he was already thinking of leaving.

Allowing herself to hope for anything more would be absurd. They were from different worlds, and chance had brought them together. Life had viciously taught her that dreams didn't come true.

"Are you listening to me?"

"Excellent advice, Garrett."

He raised one eyebrow. "That wasn't agreement."

Rather than responding, she sat to slide her shoes back on. "Tiramisu?"

CHAPTER SIX

HAWKEYE

What the fuck was he thinking?

Garrett pumped iron in the workout area of the condominium complex where he was staying.

Last night, with Charlotte, he'd crossed a line. Not that there was a rulebook for getting close to a protectee who didn't know she had a bodyguard.

Early this morning, he'd headed for the coffee shop in town, hoping to see her. But she hadn't left the ranch.

Did that mean she'd slept badly like she often did? Busy with work? Had their time together soothed her? Or had it left her uncertain?

After he arrived home, he hadn't been able to resist sending her a text message, telling her he was serious about her taking a bath.

She hadn't replied.

An hour later, frustrated, he called to check on her. Instead of answering, she sent a text maybe ten minutes later.

It was a smile emoji. Which told him…nothing. Agitation had crawled through him, and he'd checked in with the surveillance team way more than they liked.

Yesterday he'd thought the job couldn't possibly be more frustrating. He'd been wrong.

Being with her, having her in his arms, hearing her contented purrs as he spanked her shapely ass...

Yeah. He'd crossed a line all right.

Playing with submissives at a club was one thing. He'd done that in cities and towns all around the world. Giving a sub what she needed emotionally, physically was a worthy pursuit, one he enjoyed. Yet there was so much more to it with Charlotte.

She was a guarded person by nature, or maybe because life taught her to be. And he liked her, enjoyed matching wits with her. But more, he respected her. She'd opened herself to him in ways he suspected she didn't with others. He'd been honored to be the recipient of her trust.

Even if he didn't deserve it.

After repping out one last set, he headed back to his place to shower. He'd already consumed a gallon and a half of coffee while waiting for her, so he didn't need more.

Garrett turned on the cold shower knob and stood beneath the brutal mountain water, exhaling his frustration.

He'd given her what she asked for. And he'd been so in tune with her that he knew how deep to take her.

Before they'd started, he told her he couldn't promise that it wouldn't mean anything to him. That had been his instinct warning him of danger, and he'd recklessly plowed right past it as if he were a bull charging at a red flag.

Then he'd cupped her ass, and she'd settled. He cupped her ass, blocking out everything to ensure her satisfaction.

And that was the line.

It had meant something to him. He cared for her, wanted her to be happy. As a protective agent that was the absolute worst position to be in.

He'd gladly give his life for her if it came to it, but the emotion might give him blind spots.

He was already in too deep. And the problem was, even if an exit ramp existed, he wouldn't take it.

There was a team meeting at the Walker ranch at eleven. He owed it to his fellow agents to let them know what had happened. Within reason that respected her privacy. And that came with its own set of risks. Hawkeye could fire him.

But would he?

They were already a week deep into his mission, and getting Charlotte to trust someone else wouldn't be easy. Mira had tried to strike up a conversation yesterday at the fitness center, but Charlotte had politely declined chitchat and readjusted her earbuds as she headed for the elliptical machine.

Garrett finished his shower, then dressed.

Though he'd checked with the surveillance team a while ago, he sent another request for an update.

Right as he was heading out, Inamorata called. The woman was a force of nature and Hawkeye's second-in-command. She was brusque, no nonsense, and kickass at her job.

When he answered, she wasted no time on preliminaries.

"As you requested, your two new surveillance teams are being deployed. They'll be on the ground at 1300 tomorrow. The ones rotating out will be on a flight at 1700."

"Got it." Two men had volunteered to stay on, but he'd try to get them each some downtime.

"What's your sitrep?"

"I've gotten inside the Connelly ranch."

She waited.

Fuck. He shifted uncomfortably as if he were a kid who'd been sent to the principal's office. He could gloss over facts. But if Charlotte mentioned anything to her dad about

Garrett, things wouldn't be easier for him. "And close to our protectee."

"How close?" Inamorata's question was clipped.

"Not intimate." But he couldn't promise that wouldn't happen.

"Are you able to perform your job responsibilities?"

What the hell kind of question was that. "I would have resigned already if I couldn't."

"As expected. The alarm system needs to be upgraded, and Ms. Connelly keeps postponing it."

"I'll take care of it." If she ever invited him back.

"We could use another couple of cameras on the home's exterior."

"I'll get a ladder."

"I'm certain you'll figure something out. Be creative."

Without saying goodbye, she ended the call.

And he got to work. There was a job to do. Operation Snowfall was his responsibility. He'd never failed in a protective mission. He'd be damned sure that Charlotte wasn't the first.

Since the drive to the Walker ranch took some time, he left. But before backing out of his parking spot, he sent her a text.

Missed you at the coffee shop. Hope you're okay.

She didn't respond, but the message switched from *Delivered* to *Read*, and she still hadn't replied by the time he arrived at Jacob's.

This time the hissing, back-arched cat only terrified him a little. And he gave the terror a wide berth.

Elissa answered the door and saw him huddled against the railing. "She terrorizing you?" With a grin she scooped up the animal.

"No. No. She's lovely. An angel." He extended his hand toward Waffle, and she hissed. "Nice kitty."

"She'll warm up. Maybe you could feed her later?"

He looked at the feline. "Yeah. Sure."

"Come on in. Coffee's ready."

And so were croissant sandwiches. "You've got to stop spoiling us. We're going to expect this on every job."

"You deserve it."

Though he should reach for something healthier, these looked beyond delicious. Then he frowned as he selected not one, but two.

Jacob was already in the dining room, mug of coffee nearby. "How's the job?"

Because he knew Jacob had been Elissa's protective agent, Garrett was more forthcoming than he might be otherwise. "We bonded over a discussion of the portrait Elissa donated."

"I see."

"Crossed a line."

Jacob took a drink. "You know what you're doing?"

He sure as hell hoped so.

Elissa joined them. "We're having a small gathering tomorrow night at my parent's brewpub." She exchanged glances with Jacob. "We'd like you to be there. Feel free to bring Charlotte."

That idea had potential. Charlotte and Elissa—while not close friends—were more than acquaintances. Going out with a group of friends might appeal to her. "I'll see what I can do."

Torin and Mira arrived, followed by the second-shift surveillance team. Third shift was catching some shut-eye.

Garrett started with a brief update of the flight schedule. "Headquarters will be sending you boarding passes. I'll need you to brief the new arrivals."

"Roger that." One of the surveillance agents nodded.

"We'll be working on getting Ms. Connelly's security system updated and additional cameras installed."

Torin frowned. "Any plan on how you're going to do that, boss?"

"Working on it. Questions?"

Mira raised her hand. "Tomorrow's Saturday. Are we keeping the same schedule?"

"Needing your beauty sleep, Araceli?" one of the agents teased.

"Easy for you to say. You've been getting up at noon every day."

The two agents exchanged a glance. "Eleven."

"Yeah. Eleven," the other confirmed.

"In answer to the question…" Garrett projected his voice. "We don't know if her schedule changes much, if at all." And she struck him as so regimented that he wouldn't be surprised if she kept up her routine. "Go to the Sterling at the usual time."

Mira groaned. "I'll be at their coffee bar until someone notifies me she's on the way."

On the table his phone vibrated. Charlotte. Finally.

Sorry. Was in a meeting. I'm fine. Have a good day!

Garrett scowled ferociously. Maybe what they'd shared last night was a bigger mistake than he'd realized. If he'd fucked up this mission—or worse, caused her any upset—he'd never forgive himself.

When she had Garrett over for dinner, Charlotte had been able to convince herself that it wasn't a date.

But seeing him this afternoon, going to Elissa's parents' restaurant with a small group of people, was definitely a date.

And her nerves were shredded.

Maybe they wouldn't have been if she hadn't given in to her needs and the moment.

At the auction, when she'd seen his name on the bid sheet, she'd looked over her shoulder to see him watching her. There'd been a spark of recognition—submissive to Dominant—and it had been both thrilling and scary. And maybe, just maybe, inevitable.

Then Thursday evening in the great room, his comments about the meaning of the portrait had proven they were in tune with each other. Each had something to give as well as receive.

She'd turned herself over to him, and she'd received much more than she had dared dream. He'd been as kind as he was masterful as if he instinctively knew the reasons she wanted the spanking. It wasn't really for pain or pleasure or even the act of submission itself. Instead it was a way to truly let go, not think about the myriad work details that were always clamoring for her attention. Even the pain of Andy's betrayal disappeared.

Garrett had made her feel special. When he swept his gaze over her, his eyes darkened with appreciation that couldn't be faked.

And that was the real problem.

She liked him. Too much.

It wasn't just his charm or good looks though he had those in abundance. It was more about how easy it was to be with him. At the end of the evening, she hadn't wanted him to leave, and that scared her. At most, they had days, maybe a week or two, together. Then she'd have to deal with never seeing him again.

To prevent future hurt, she'd tried to put some distance between them.

The attempt hadn't worked.

His texts and calls had been regular though not often

enough to make her uncomfortable. But they did make her heart momentarily stop. And they made her happy.

The invite to join him this afternoon had been tempting. Still, she hesitated. Then Elissa had called personally, saying how much she hoped to see Charlotte.

The online buzz about Finnegan's Pub was positive. All the things that people had loved about the original Conroy's in Denver had been replicated here, but the menu had been expanded, and they brewed their own beer.

As much as she loved her house, the walls were closing in on her, especially since she wasn't going to town as often as she liked. Work was keeping her busy. Staying home was also a way to ensure she didn't run in to Garrett.

Getting out and seeing people she enjoyed appealed to her. She had friends who had second homes up here, but they weren't arriving until later in the season. Charlotte truly did like Elissa. Jacob she hadn't spent much time with, but he'd been charming at the fundraiser.

If she said yes, that also meant she had to spend time with Garrett.

Her mind shouted *no*. Her renegade heart whispered *yes*.

In the end she'd grabbed a yellow legal pad and made a list of pros and cons.

Though there were more cons, the fact they wouldn't be alone at her house had been the deciding factor. They could meet downtown, and then she could drive home afterward.

Garrett, however, was having none of that.

"Gentlemen don't behave that way. Besides, my mother would..."

Once he'd made her laugh, she'd been helpless to resist him.

This time she expected him to be early, so she planned accordingly. Because it might snow later, she wore leggings and heeled boots. They might not be practical, but they were stylish. She reassured herself she wasn't trying to impress him. But his comment about her pumps played around in the back of her mind.

When he arrived, she opened the gate, smoothing the front of her leggings. She was ready but giddy with excitement.

Minutes later she opened the door and waited for him to reach the porch.

Instead of entering the house right away, he stopped. Sunlight danced off the raven strands of his hair, and he smelled of fresh mountain air.

Lazy in his perusal, he swept his gaze over her, seeming to take in every single detail. "You look amazing."

As always, he was quick with compliments. Despite the fact she was prepared for them, they still packed an emotionally powerful punch. "Thank you."

The sight of him took her breath away. His jeans looked as if he'd been poured into them. His broad shoulders filled out his leather jacket, and his soft gray Henley shirt hugged his torso. It had three buttons, all fastened, all encouraging her to open them, one by one.

"Those boots..." He tipped his head to the side. "Are they for me?"

She told him what she'd told herself. "It's supposed to snow."

"Yeah." His wide, fast grin told her he hadn't bought her response. "I can appreciate how practical they are."

Caught. Embarrassment heated her cheek.

"I've been looking forward to seeing you since Thursday."

A purposeful glint darkened his eyes, rocking her. He took a step closer to her, rocking her world. In this moment, he was a total alpha—in charge and in control.

"I'm going to kiss you, Charlotte."

Letting him come here was a mistake. When she was

close to him, her body betrayed her completely. This was a dance, and she wanted him to lead.

"May I come in?"

She stepped back. Within seconds they were in the foyer, and he'd slammed the door shut.

"Tell me not to do this..." His voice was ragged with demand. "Say that I'm wrong about the attraction between us."

Charlotte worried her lower lip. "You're not wrong."

"I missed you."

In the face of his honesty, how could she be anything but brave? "Same."

"Did you?"

As her pulse fluttered, she nodded.

"I thought about you constantly."

Her breaths became a little more jagged.

"Holding you. Touching you. *Pleasing you.*"

More than any other man ever had. That, she realized, was what terrified her the most. When she visited the Reserve, the Tops she'd played with had been extraordinarily skilled. But she'd been one of a number of bottoms they'd played with that night. To them, she was interchangeable with anyone else. There was no emotional connection.

Two years ago, she'd met Andy and had been swept up in their whirlwind romance. He had no interest in BDSM, and he'd made it clear that he didn't want her going to the club without him.

It was an exchange she was willing to make. A husband at her side, the promise of family.

On that terrible night when they'd ended things for good, he'd hurled vicious words at her, and they'd found their target. Since then she hadn't had the inclination to visit the Reserve.

Garrett threaded his fingers into her hair and leaned in closer, and she tipped back her head in invitation.

He accepted, taking charge. Expression intense, he backed her against the wall, trapping her there, pinning her arms above her.

"I didn't sleep last night." His eyes were as dark and turbulent as a storm-tossed sea.

Then he leaned in a little more until his masculine, Dominant presence overwhelmed her senses.

"What did you do to me, woman?"

Catching her off guard, he grabbed hold of the hem of her sweater, then pulled it up, baring her abdomen. Slowly, with agonizingly gentle strokes, he covered her abdomen, moving up.

Her nipples beaded. He didn't go farther though she wouldn't have stopped him if he did.

Instead he retraced the path he'd taken, continuing down, over the waistband of her leggings. Then he slowed his touch, stopping at her pubic bone.

Her pussy throbbed.

As if he were a master of seduction, he played her perfectly. Desperately she spread her thighs.

Garrett eased his hand a fraction of an inch away from her body and moved his fingers lower. Then he glanced the barest of touches over her pussy.

In frustration she moaned. It wasn't possible to be any more turned on than she was in this moment.

"You're passionate."

He captured her mouth, demanding entrance.

Immediately, completely, she gave him what he wanted.

The other night had been a prelude, but this was breathtaking. He swirled his tongue around hers in a beautiful entreaty before delving deeper.

With as much patience as skill, he made love with his

tongue, coaxing her response until she was molten, tongues melding.

He worked his free hand behind her, biting his fingers into her buttocks as he brought her closer to him.

The zing of pain—a contrast to his sensual kiss—weakened her knees. Instantly he tightened his grip on her wrists, offering complete support.

With a moan, she jutted her hips forward. His cock was hard and ready, and he deepened the kiss, their tongues frantically tangling as lovemaking became raw dominance.

He was all but fucking her mouth, and she was begging for more, meeting his thrusts with parries of her own. She'd never experienced passion like this.

By slow measures, he ended the kiss, but before releasing her completely, he gently bit her lower lip, leaving behind a delicious sting.

"You taste like forever."

Surely she'd misheard him.

"If we have any hope of making it to the restaurant in time, I have to stop." His eyes smoldered, and he sucked in a breath as he released his grip on her rear, then her wrists.

After he helped her to lower her arms, he massaged the small marks he'd left behind.

"Thank you." She appreciated that he knew her so well. She yearned for strength but needed it to be tempered with gentleness.

"There's more to come."

Her thoughts whirled with the possibilities his tone promised.

"If you want it."

"Very much."

The hem of her sweater was caught in the waistband of her leggings, and he untucked it. "Are you ready?"

"I need to grab my jacket from the coat closet. And I'm afraid my hair may need to be tamed."

"And you may want a fresh coat of lipstick." His eyes danced. "But be warned. It'll be a temptation I'm not sure I can resist."

Truthfully she wasn't sure it was a temptation she wanted him to resist. "Give me five minutes."

"Any longer and I might come check on you."

Heeding his warning, she hurried upstairs.

Several minutes later, she was still repairing the damage to her makeup and hair. Once she was put together, she grinned at her reflection. Even if they were a few minutes late, the kiss was worth it.

When she returned to the main level, he was in the sunroom, looking outside.

Either sensing her presence or because of the strike of her heels on the tile, he turned.

"You were right about the view. And the patio is spectacular."

It was covered with a massive, sharply angled roof constructed from hand-hewn logs. There was a fireplace. The outdoor kitchen saw little use, and all the pieces were covered for the season.

"Hot tub?"

"I rarely use it. But it's pretty magical when it snows." Which was in the forecast. "A glass of wine and the contrast of heat and cold. Well, it's perfect except for the dash back inside when you're done."

"Hopefully you have a nice fluffy robe?"

By unspoken accord, they walked toward the foyer where she grabbed her fluffy parka. She started to slip an arm into a sleeve but stopped when he cleared his throat.

Shaking her head, she met his gaze. "Let me guess. Your mother also insisted you hold a woman's coat for her?"

"Manners are a gentleman's best friend."

"I can't argue with that." Besides, he would win.

He was the perfect assistant, even scooping her hair off her back and shoulders.

"Shall we?"

She picked up her purse from the small side table. "Ready."

Garrett opened the door, then paused to indicate the panel on the wall. "You're not setting the alarm? Or do you control it from your phone?"

"It's daylight." And the property was protected by a fence line and the gate.

"Bad things only happen at night?"

"Now you sound like my dad."

"He does have a point. It's remote out here. It would take a while for police to respond if something ever happened."

"Nothing ever has."

"In an emergency, every moment counts. And the best incident is one that never occurs."

"Spoken like a military man?"

"The element of surprise can work for you or against you."

When she didn't respond, he lifted one shoulder in an easy shrug. "Humor me."

Because there was no reason not to, she pushed the series of buttons.

"Thank you. Promise me you'll always keep it set, even when you're home."

Tipping her head to one side, she considered him. "Are you always so protective?"

"Protecting the country and its citizens is in my veins."

After the front door was closed, he cupped her arm as they descended the steps. Then he settled her into the luxurious comfort of his SUV.

"Switch for the seat warmer is right there." He pointed to a spot on the dash.

At the moment she was fine. Being near him seemed to increase her internal temperature by several degrees.

A few minutes later, they were on the road leading into downtown.

"Do you want to choose some music?"

"What do you prefer?"

"Lady's choice."

"Seriously?" Andy always blasted classic rock. More than once she'd suspected it was so they didn't have to have a conversation.

Garrett picked up his phone. "Samantha, unlock screen."

A soft female voice responded. *"Okay, Garrett. Unlocked. What else can I do for you?"*

"Impressive."

"Bonds technology. A little AI built in there."

Which reminded her of the Workflow acquisition. She wanted to get that deal done, and if it didn't happen, they needed to acquire something else. "No fingerprint or passcode?"

"I've got those as a backup. But voice control can be handy."

"I'm waiting, Garrett."

"So impatient." He glanced at Charlotte. "What's your choice?"

"I'm going out on a limb. How about something Irish? To get us into the spirit."

"Anything in particular?"

She grinned. "The 'Unicorn' song."

He raised a skeptical eyebrow.

"You know, green alligators and long-necked geese and such."

"Why not?" He pushed a button on the steering wheel. "The lady would like to hear the 'Unicorn' song."

"Now playing the 'Unicorn' by the Irish Rovers."

As Charlotte sang along, horrendously offkey, he laughed.

She scowled indignantly. "Just for that, you have to sing with me."

He shook his head. "I'm lousy."

"Didn't stop me."

When they reached the chorus again, he joined in. "Your voice isn't horrible at all. I think that was a fib."

"It's only because you do not have a discerning ear. I assure you, that was dreadful."

He stopped at an intersection, and they exchanged glances before laughing.

"What's so funny, Garrett?"

"The limits of AI. Nuance can be missed, but Bonds keeps rolling out upgrades to make it better. Of course, it's difficult because he doesn't always understand them himself."

By the time they listened to a couple more tracks from the studio album, they reached the restaurant. Despite it being midafternoon and plenty of people were likely on the slopes, the parking lot was packed.

She waited for him to open her door.

"Very good." In a seductive purr, he whispered the words against her ear, and a chill rocked her.

"Since you're already in the spirit, are you having a Guinness while we're here?"

"Of course." She shook her head in disbelief as if the question were absurd. "What other kind of beer is there?"

He laughed. "A woman after my own heart."

An overhead bell danced as they entered the restaurant.

Festive music spilled from the speakers, and the place buzzed with laughter and conversation. A grinning leprechaun was drawn on the blackboard. He wore a tall green hat and sported an apron bearing the name Finnegan's. Specials of the day were listed beneath, and they all sounded delicious.

"That's it." Garrett nodded. "I don't need to look at the menu. Shephard's pie for me."

She grinned. "I'll eat anything as long as mashed potatoes are involved."

Before they had a chance to look for their party, Elissa hurried toward them. She gave them each a great big hug and welcomed them to the pub. "We have a snug in the back."

Charlotte and Garrett exchanged glances.

"What?" he asked.

They made their way through the place, dodging servers with massive trays of food and drink.

"Since it's not a separate room, it's not a traditional snug. But we have a large cozy booth with a partition for privacy." She led the way past it. "Everyone, this is Garrett Young and Charlotte Connelly."

A little girl looked up from her drawing but quickly lowered her head.

Jacob stood to shake hands with Garrett and to greet Charlotte.

"Hello!" An older woman waved them over. Elissa's mother no doubt. She scooted closer to the man on her left.

Because the table was a half-circle, it was easy to see and converse with everyone.

"My parents and owners of this fine establishment...my mom, Ann."

Ann patted the seat next to her. "Come sit with us."

"And my dad, Patrick." He lifted his beer in acknowledgment.

As the final introductions were performed, Charlotte slid in next to Patrick, and Garrett followed her. With that many people, it definitely was snug.

"Badass ski champion and children's book author extraordinaire, Deborah."

"Exaggerations." She shook her head. "But this is why I love Elissa."

"And her little girl, budding illustrator, Adele."

When she didn't look up, her mother gently nudged her. Adele carried on as if not noticing.

"What are you drawing?" Charlotte asked.

The youngster picked up her piece of paper. There was a cat, remarkable in its detail.

"Waffle."

"The Maine Coon stray who adopted us," Jacob explained.

"I named her." Adele smiled for the first time. "She's got a lot of browns. And her nose is white. It looks like whipped cream."

"I think your picture is spectacular." Charlotte seemed genuinely enthused. "Lots of detail."

Garrett spoke up. "I've never seen that creature look so pleasant."

Adele smiled. "She must not like you."

Deborah gasped. "I'm sorry."

Jacob laughed. "She's got you there, buddy, old friend."

A server came laden with one of the biggest trays Charlotte had ever seen.

"I hope you don't mind." Ann beamed. "We took the liberty of preparing a lot of our specialties so that you can have a taste of everything."

This wasn't a taste. It was a feast.

The server named the dishes as she placed them on the table. "For the young lady, chicken strips. And for everyone, shepherd's pie. Irish soda bread. Fish and chips. Made with cod. Mushy peas. Corned beef. Bangers and mash." Following that was some traditional bar favorites: nachos, potato skins loaded with everything, and Irish cheese dip. "Don't drive after eating this stuff!"

Patrick chuckled. "Plenty of beer and whiskey in there."

Even if they ate for a week, they would never make it through this mountain of food.

Before she left, the server addressed Charlotte and Garrett. "What can I get you to drink?"

They responded at the same time. "Guinness."

"Can I interest you in our house stout? I think you might like it."

"It's a new recipe from our brewmaster." Patrick lifted his pint. "If the taste doesn't suit you, you can send it back."

The server nodded. "Or I'm happy to bring a sample."

"Better yet, lass." Patrick nodded. "And another for me."

"Anyone else?"

"Make it another round," Jacob said.

The tasters arrived while the plates were being passed around.

Garrett nodded. "I like it."

"Same." Charlotte agreed.

"I'll be right back."

She returned with drinks, and then the food.

Throughout the meal, Adele barely ate, but she held up each picture as she finished it.

Charlotte took a bite of mashed potatoes. "I may have died and gone to heaven."

Ann grinned. "My mother's recipe."

"It's amazing." Though she shouldn't, Charlotte scooped some more onto her plate. "Your brewpub is wonderful. And busy for this time of day."

"We couldn't be happier here."

"Even though you sold Conroy's to slow down," Elissa teased.

Patrick spoke up. "Well, we're doing better at being owners instead of doing all the work."

Ann continued the explanation. "We were going to buy a cabin, but we found a home we loved, and it was move-in ready. So we needed something to occupy our time until Elissa has wee ones."

Charlotte glanced at Elissa.

"We're hoping for four," Ann finished.

Jacob cleared his throat. "About that…" He glanced at Elissa. "We've been engaged for a while. Elissa has finally agreed to set a date."

Cheers exploded around the table, and Deborah clapped. Ann pressed her hands to her heart as her eyes filled with tears.

"About time." Patrick took a drink.

Jacob picked up Elissa's hand. "Tell them when."

She gave a twisted smile. "Next month. Sorry, Mom."

"Next month?"

"We're having the ceremony at the ranch. And it will be just a handful of people. We want to be sure you all will be there."

Patrick nodded. "We'll handle the catering."

Beneath the table, Garrett touched Charlotte's leg.

"And I need to find a dress," Elissa said.

Deborah and Anne both volunteered for that responsibility.

The next hour passed in a crazy blur as the couple shared their plans and everyone discussed the details.

Garrett ordered a bottle of champagne, and when it arrived, proposed a toast. "To the love you have found—with gratitude for being an inspiration to the rest of us."

"Slainte!" Patrick called.

Among the cheers, Garrett turned to Charlotte. "Would you like to go to the wedding with me?"

She was honored to be included in Jacob and Elissa's celebration, and maybe she shouldn't be surprised that Garrett asked her to attend with him. This afternoon was definitely a date, but going to that kind of event together seemed like something an established couple did together. And yet she wanted to go with him even though she shouldn't. "Yes."

He smiled as he squeezed her thigh just a little.

A bounty of desserts arrived, including a cake made with the house stout beer. It was delectable, but she couldn't eat more than one bite.

The server returned to ask if there was anything else they needed.

Garrett leaned over to whisper in her ear. "The only thing I need is to get you home as soon as possible."

Maybe it was the conversation about the wedding, the talk of babies, or the way his voice held a rough, seductive edge, but everything inside her softened. She couldn't think of anything she wanted more, even though she knew where it would lead.

CHAPTER SEVEN

HAWKEYE

Once they were inside her house, Garrett turned on the lights, then closed the door and locked it before setting the alarm.

"You're good at that."

"They're pretty well all the same."

He turned toward her, then looked at her, his green eyes gleaming with the purposeful intent she recognized.

"Where were we?"

Warmth unfurled through her when he plucked her purse from her shoulder and placed it on the side table.

Next he slowly unzipped her parka.

Charlotte had never experienced anyone like Garrett. He was sensual and determined, sexy in his dominance as he removed her jacket. But instead of discarding it, he hung it back in the closet. Each of his movements stretched her nerves tighter and tighter.

"Now I'm remembering." He took a step toward her, then a second.

Instinctively she backed up.

As if he had her where he wanted her, he grinned, quickly

pinning her against the wall. "Yeah. This is where we were." He fisted his hand into her hair, imprisoning her while he devoured her mouth, bringing her back to full arousal.

Like he had earlier, he lifted the hem of her sweater. Then he drew a fingertip from the bottom of her bra to the top of her leggings.

Unlike earlier, he did not pull his hand away. Instead he hooked his thumbs into her waistband and drew her leggings down over her hipbones. "Keep your hands against the wall."

She desperately wanted to grab hold of him.

"You'll do as you're told, won't you?"

Damn him. She nodded.

"Tell me what I want to hear, Charlotte. I love the sound of your capitulation."

"Yes." The word was hiss, a whisper, a promise. "Yes, Sir."

With a growl he dropped to his knees and continued to pull her leggings down to her knees. She was desperate to be out of the material to give him access. As it was, they were more bondage than anything. And he no doubt knew it.

After dampening one of his fingertips, he slid it between her feminine folds.

"All day, this is where I've wanted to be." He parted her labia so he could tease her clit with his tongue. It was far too much sensation and simultaneously not enough.

He stopped to look up at her.

It took all of her self-control to remain in position, waiting on his will.

Garrett began to play with her again, keeping their gazes locked as he slid a finger inside her.

With a sharp gasp, she jerked.

"Is this what you want?"

A million times, yes.

"Maybe this...?"

Easing her apart, he slid a second finger in her.

"Garrett." She clenched her buttocks as an orgasm built.

"Hmm?"

"I need…" It had been so very long for her. Her vibrator didn't compensate for human touch, the intimate exploration.

"What? What do you need, beautiful Charlotte?"

"I'm ready to come."

He touched his thumb to her clit. "Not yet."

"But…"

"Distract yourself?"

The harder she tried, the more the desire claimed her.

"What's your favorite recipe?"

"What?"

"Pie? Cake? Bread?"

"Have you lost your mind?"

Still lazily exploring her, he laughed. "Trying to make you lose yours."

She tried to think, but her mind spiraled. "Garrett?"

On some level she was aware of him speaking to her, but then he licked her again, and she was lost, tapping her heels frantically as she fought the inevitable.

Seconds later a million sensations swirled in her and a climax dragged her under its potent spell, but he was there for her, his free hand on her torso. "Hold on to my shoulders."

Before she'd completely recovered, he scooped her up and carried her to the large couch in the great room. He settled himself onto the couch and pulled her on to his lap.

Mindless of her awkward state of undress, Charlotte curled into him, her cheek pressed against his shirt, until her breathing evened out. "That was…"

"An appetizer?" he suggested with a hint of laughter in his tone.

"Your jokes are ridiculous. You know that, right?"

"I shouldn't pursue a career in comedy?"

"Please don't." As a lover, though, he was amazing.

For long minutes they remained where they were. She wasn't sure she'd ever been this comfortable with a man before.

Eventually she placed a hand against his chest and pushed herself back slightly, enough that she could look at his gorgeous face and take in his satisfied smile.

"Are you ready for the main course?"

"Stop." Though she protested, they both laughed.

The muffled sound of her phone ringing reached her.

"Do you need to get that?" Garrett loosened his grip on her.

She wiggled her leggings back into place. "It's probably work. Bradley, if my guess is right."

"Bradley?"

"A senior member of our management team."

"At this time on a Saturday?"

"He's an overachiever. Smart—Ivy League Education with an MBA. His brain is only matched by his vision and ambitiousness. I have a lot of respect for him. The problem is, I don't think he knows what a weekend is." She gave a half-laugh. "He's been texting all day." Not that that was unusual. Most times she was glad to answer because it also gave her something to do.

But not today. Before leaving, she'd said she would be at an event but expected to be home by five or six. He'd asked her to get back with him when she could, and she promised she would. It would be nice to have a few undisturbed hours to herself. "We're in the middle of a couple of big things going on right now. An acquisition that my dad has slowed down on, and he wants a preliminary draft of a succession plan to be done by the end of the year."

"Sounds complicated."

"It is. Lots of things to think about and discuss. It will set the path for the future of the company. Who are we grooming? And for what positions? What needs to be in place for the time when my dad wants to retire?"

"Is that imminent?"

"No. Thank goodness." At least she didn't think so. But Bradley's comment about Malcolm seeming tired had stuck with her.

Before leaving for the brewpub, she'd called her dad, and he again reassured her he was fine and told her to stop worrying.

Aware that Garrett was looking at her, waiting for her to go on, she shook her head. "No. He's still young. In my ideal world, he's going to be running Connelly and Company well into his eighties." She brushed hair back from face. "I think he's pushing so hard because his own dad died of a heart attack at fifty-eight."

"How old is your dad?"

"Fifty-seven."

He nodded.

"To be honest with you, I don't even like thinking about it even though I know any plan we come up with is flexible and gives us a path forward. Kind of goes hand-in-hand with long-term planning."

"Makes sense."

"Bradley's spearheading the project, primarily because I was dragging my feet. And I don't want to see my name in the owner or CEO positions." She grinned. "Maybe I should be more appreciative of Bradley's efforts. He'll get the report done on time, if not early, and that will make us both look good."

"Sounds like a handy teammate to have."

"You're right." Her phone went silent. *But for how long?*

Almost instantly her ring tone shattered the building

silence. "Sorry. If I were sure it was Bradley, I'd ignore it." But it could be her father.

"I'm guessing he's going to continue to call until you answer."

She laughed. "No doubt."

"You'd better get it."

"If you'll excuse me? After I handle this, I'll turn off the phone."

Garrett's eyes darkened. "I'm not going anywhere."

A thrill danced through her, but that burst of excitement vanished when she picked up the demanding device and saw Bradley's name on the caller identification screen. Sending him to voicemail might give her momentary satisfaction, but she'd be forced to deal with him at some point.

On the fourth and final ring, she swiped the button to answer the summons. "Evening, Bradley."

"Char." He exhaled. "Finally. I was worried about you."

"My event was a lot of fun, and I just got home. What's up?"

"Been working all day, and I've got some ideas for the succession plan."

Of course he did. "That's awesome."

"Figured we could go over them together."

"Let's do it Monday."

He fell silent.

With a sigh, she relented. "Tomorrow afternoon, then."

Garrett stood and crossed the room to switch on the fireplace, instantly creating ambiance. She was anxious to get back to him and continue what they'd started.

With a deep sigh, Bradley relented. "How about ten o'clock?"

She wasn't sure whether Garrett was planning to spend the night. They hadn't talked about it. And he was a gentleman enough not to assume. Did that mean she should invite him?

As if sensing her thoughts were focused on him, he turned to face her. He took her in, grinning wickedly.

"Char?"

If Garrett stayed, she didn't want him to feel obligated to leave early. And brunch in the sunroom would be divine.

"Char!"

"I'm miles away. Sorry."

"Is everything okay?"

"It is. Thanks for your concern. Two o'clock tomorrow?" By then, surely she'd be ready to focus on work.

"Ten's better for me."

"I might be tied up then." Well, with luck she would be.

Garrett chuckled.

"Two o'clock." She nodded. "I'll call you." Without going through the usual goodbye pleasantries, she ended the call, then switched off the device and dropped it back in her purse.

The act was more satisfying than she imagined.

Her boots clicking on the floor, she purposefully strode back to where Garrett was now seated on the couch.

Boldly she straddled him, and his gorgeous eyes widened with approval. "So..." She placed her hands on his shoulders. "Where were we?"

"I'm not sure I remember." His voice was gruff, ultramasculine. Beyond sexy. "Why don't you remind me?"

"Why don't I?" It was a little out of her comfort zone to be the aggressor, but his smile emboldened her.

She leaned forward to brush a kiss across his lips.

Then she feathered her fingers into his thick hair, giving in to the temptation that had been teasing her since the first time she'd seen him on the gondola. "I like you with messy hair."

"Likewise."

Following a pattern he'd established, she fisted his shirt and tugged it up from the bottom to expose his abdomen. *Holy crap.* "Damn, Sir."

She'd guessed that he worked out, but he was ripped.

"I grab a quick workout when I can."

Charlotte spent enough time in the fitness center to know better. No one got a body like this from lifting a few casual weights. It spoke of discipline in everything he did, from eating to exercise.

Desperate to reveal more, she released the buttons to tug the long-sleeved shirt over his head, revealing a honed chest that had the perfect smattering of hair. *It should be a crime to keep that body under wraps.*

His biceps were enormous, and she'd already taken comfort from their tender strength.

With a purr, she linked her arms behind his head and pressed her mouth to his, asking, then taking.

For thirty seconds, maybe a little more, he allowed her to lead, and then the natural order of things reasserted itself, and he took over, tasting her while promising so much more.

Demandingly his cock pressed against her.

When reality receded to the point there was only the two of them on the planet, he ended the kiss.

"Woman..." His voice was hoarse with desire.

"Why, Mr. Logan. I do believe your memory is returning."

"I need to get you upstairs before I take you over the back of the couch."

"Really?"

His grin sent shockwaves through her.

"You'd like that, would you?"

Where had this new, bolder version of her come from? "I might."

"We'll find out later."

Thrilling her, his words sounded more like an intention than a question.

He clamped his hands on her waist, then moved her back, then held her until she was steady on her feet. "I have other ideas for you first."

Butterflies—some from nerves, others from anticipation—became a flurry inside her.

"Lead on."

She took a step back, and he stood, snatching up his shirt as he did.

As she walked in front of him, she was aware of his hot gaze on her rear.

"Damn. I love the way your hips sway when you walk."

Over her shoulder, she shot him a come-hither look.

"You'll pay for that."

Yes, please.

She reached the first step of the staircase and curled her hand around the banister. Then she took her time climbing.

"Those fucking boots…"

God. His approval fed something deep insider her, something ignored for so long that she didn't even realize it was starving.

Once they were inside her massive room with its vaulted ceiling, he shut the door behind them. It sealed with a decisive click. *Now what?*

Downstairs, she'd been confident in her role as an aggressor, but now she was soft and weak for him.

"Do you have any toys?"

The question was personal, and myriad possibilities for their evening unfurled. "What do you have in mind?"

"A paddle, perhaps?"

Aware of him watching her, she walked to her closet.

"Something not too harsh."

With hands that were a little shaky, she opened the built-in drawers. Since she couldn't decide which he might prefer, she selected two.

When she returned to the bedroom, he'd moved her wing back chair and small table away from the wall.

He sat there, all fierce and expectant. "Bring them to me."

Slowly, aware of the powershift as she entered a more submissive mindset, she crossed the room and came to a stop in front of him.

"You may kneel."

It wasn't more than a request. It was as if he'd known that the desire crossed her mind but that she wasn't sure he wanted that.

"You've got perfect instincts. Trust them. I will never be disappointed with you, Charlotte. You can't get it wrong."

The combination of her heels and holding onto the paddles made her a little awkward, and he reached to assist her.

"Exquisite."

She basked in his approval. Then she offered him the implements that brought as much pleasure as pain.

He accepted them and considered each in turn. "The wooden one will leave you with too many marks."

But its hollow sound was so very satisfying.

"This one will do."

The leather was a jewel-toned green, reminding her of his eyes.

"We can use it for much longer."

He knew what she wanted as well as needed.

"How about vibrators?" He placed the paddles on the small table. "Something insertable. Perhaps that has a remote control?"

"A few. But I've never played like that."

"Show me."

He helped her to stand, but when she returned to the closet, he followed her.

Heat rocked through her body as she opened a drawer.

"Options for days." Rather than any teasing note, his voice contained approval. "Do you have a preference?"

"The egg."

"Why?"

"It's uhm…" She wanted to hide.

Waiting for an answer, he remained where he was.

"Big, and the buzz is pretty wonderful."

He extended his palm, and she picked up the vibrator and gave it to him. "How many settings does it have?"

"I don't know. Seven maybe?" She had set it to medium and left it there.

"And the remote?"

She picked up the little device.

"Go ahead and turn it on."

The thing looked small in his big hand, but when she adjusted the speed, it bounced and buzzed.

"Is that as high as it will go?"

"I was afraid you might ask about that." But she dutifully selected the most intense vibration.

"That'll work." He dropped a kiss on her forehead as he plucked the controller from her grip.

She followed him back to the room, and she expected him to resume his seat. Surprising her, he didn't.

Instead he spread his legs and folded his arms across his chest. The earlier, approachable man who'd taken her to a party was gone. In his place was a formidable Dominant.

"Strip for me, Charlotte."

Could he not make this easy for her? She wanted to be swept away, lost in his touch. But this set a different tone, one that made her insides molten

She bent to remove the boots. He was considerate enough to offer a hand.

"I wish there were a way to get you out of your clothes while you were still wearing those."

Next she removed her sweater and bra.

A little pulse in his temple kicked up its tempo.

"Your breasts are beautiful. And your nipples are begging me to suck them."

The words made her ache.

"Ask me to do it."

Wordlessly she cupped her breasts and offered them to him.

"Charlotte…"

"Suck them, Garrett."

Beneath his breath, he swore. Then he took one of the beaded tips into his mouth, swirling his tongue around it, elongating it, sending pleasure through her.

Heaven save her. Nothing could have prepared her for a man like him.

He took his time with each tip, leaving her breathless.

"I love how your body responds to mine."

With the spell he wove around her—Dominant to submissive—what choice did she have?

She was so ready for sex, wanting him with quiet desperation.

"Finish undressing."

Her whole body on fire, she did as he said, leaving her clothes piled on the floor. Then he scooped her up and placed her on the edge of the bed.

"You have a word for slow and one for stop."

Charlotte nodded.

"Other than that, you are mine for the night."

"There's nothing I want more."

"Good. We're in agreement." Heat blazed his eyes. "Now I

want you to lie back and place your hands beneath your back."

"Do you want me to scoot back?"

He shook his head. "I want your legs spread as far apart as you can."

Which meant she would be exposed completely to him.

"Questions?" When she didn't respond, he grinned. "Then quit stalling."

Slowly she followed his instructions.

Garrett picked up the leather paddle, and her eyes widened. He couldn't possibly mean… The word *blue* skittered around her consciousness.

"I told you to spread your legs as far as you can."

Trusting but cautious, she did.

"Wider." He tapped the insides of her thighs. "Don't make me tie you up."

"No, Sir."

"That's better." He tossed the paddle onto the bed nearby, in her peripheral vision.

He moved in closer and spread her labia.

Crying out, she arched, and she wasn't sure whether she was seeking more or trying to escape.

"Remember to keep your hands beneath you and your legs spread."

Helpless before him, she met his gaze.

He licked her labia, then teased, then knelt to eat her pussy until she was screaming his name, desperate to have him inside her. "I need you, Garrett."

"I'm not done with you yet. Come for me."

She was lost, writhing, begging, as climax after climax claimed her.

When she was overwhelmed, unable to even think, he stopped, then helped her to stand up.

This experience with him was beyond anything she imagined possible.

"I could do that all night."

She wasn't sure she could survive it. "Are we going to make love?"

"Not yet."

"I'm more than ready."

"I'll be the judge of that." With a wicked grin, he slid a finger inside her. "You're getting there."

That was a lie. She was wet and weak.

Then he found her G-spot. Eyes widening in shock, she gasped. Her knees weakened, and she grabbed him for support. "Garret, please."

"Soon." He soothed and promised. "Very soon."

Unless he took her, she'd go mad.

"I want you to bend over the bed."

Frustratingly he eased his finger from her.

Maybe because he saw how much effort it took for her to respond, he helped her into position. "Lift up your hips."

She raised onto her tiptoes, and the mattress supported her upper body. Schooling her breath, she tried to relax. Then she inhaled as he began to work the egg inside her, farther with each stroke, until he gave a final push and seated it completely.

"Let's see how this works." He delivered a gentle pulse.

It was just enough to make her aware of its presence but not enough to drive her to an orgasm.

"How is that?"

"It's…" Before she could respond, he nudged up the intensity. "Oh!" Reflexively she clenched her buttocks.

"You like that?"

"I do… But…"

"Hmm?"

"I don't think I can take it."

"Let's see, shall we?"

Once again he turned it up. "Garrett!" She was swimming, lost somewhere.

Then the paddling began, a gentle breeze on her buttocks and upper thighs and increasing as the minutes blended together. Then her skin blazed. Her vision blurred. His words came from a great distance, reassuring and loving. They caressed her as did the leather.

The egg inside her thrummed with incessant demand. "Garrett…" Did she whisper his name? Or was that her imagination?

And then her world began to spin, and her thoughts fractured. Time vanished as stars exploded behind her eyes. A shockingly powerful orgasm wrapped her in its demanding embrace. She screamed, desperate for it to never end.

As if knowing what she needed, Garrett whispered to her, and he let the vibration continue for several more seconds. Then suddenly, a second climax overtook her, making her gasp and shake.

Perspiration dotted her body, and she was on fire, from the inside out.

The sound of his voice was closer now, more insistent.

"I've got you."

While she still trembled, he removed the egg. Then he sat on the bed and pulled her into his arms. Drawing comfort from his silent support and the steady beat of his heart beneath her ear, she snuggled in close.

Long minutes later, her breathing returned to near normal, and she tipped her head back to look at him. "I'm…" *Speechless.* "That was amazing." She had no idea how many times she'd shattered, but she knew it would take some time to feel whole again.

"Now I think you're about ready."

CHAPTER EIGHT

HAWKEYE

As he moved her from his lap and onto the mattress next to him, Garrett's motions were as gentle as they were purposeful. In that moment, Charlotte realized she was falling for him no matter how ridiculous it seemed.

She hadn't known him all that long, but they had a connection unlike any she'd ever shared with anyone. He coaxed responses she hadn't known she was capable of.

That terrified her. Her reaction was too real, too consuming. Intuition flashed a bright warning, telling her to protect her heart.

She wondered though. Was it already too late?

"Give me a second." He tucked a wayward strand of hair behind her ear before leaving the bed.

Without his body heat next to her, goose bumps chased up her arms, and she adjusted her position so that she was under the covers. Then she turned on her side to watch while he removed a condom from his wallet. "Always prepared?"

"No. Actually I stopped at the drug store on my way over, just in case."

She grinned. "Did you?"

"There's a ridiculous number of choices." He tossed the package onto the nightstand, then slowly began to strip.

His body was gorgeous. And when he removed his briefs, she sucked in a breath. His cock was enormous. No wonder he told her he wanted her to be ready for him. "I hope you bought the extra-large size?"

In response to her teasing, he smiled. Then he took a step toward the bed, and his eyebrows drew together as he focused all of his attention on her.

"Garrett..."

He pulled back the covers and joined her. Gathering her close, he skimmed his fingers across her bare skin, soothing away her doubts and fears while reigniting awareness.

Then he trailed gentle kisses down her body, and lower to kiss her pussy.

Moaning, she writhed.

He swirled his tongue, licking and teasing until she cried out. Only then did he slide a finger inside her. With his gentle yet purposeful touches, he brought her back to the same state of arousal as she'd been in earlier when he'd spanked her.

"Damn, Charlotte. You're so goddamn perfect for me in every way."

How did he manage to say the most perfect thing? "I'm so ready for you."

But he continued what he was doing, watching her responses until she lifted her hips in silent invitation.

With a guttural, possessive growl, he took a moment to roll the protection into place. "I've got to have you."

"Please." She wanted nothing more.

He moved between her legs and gently stroked himself inside, a little bit at a time, making sure she was slick for him.

"Damn woman. You are so tight."

Or maybe he was just so damn big.

"Take me." His command—demand—rocked her.

She could deny him nothing. "Yes"

With a final thrust, he was balls deep, and it took her a moment to catch her breath.

He fisted her hair, holding her prisoner while he kissed her. It was nothing tender like before. This was emotional. He devoured her, destroyed her.

Then, with her lips tender and swollen, he began to move, rhythmically asking, then taking until they moved as one.

She wrapped her arms around him, holding on as he claimed her.

"You're so wet for me."

Maybe because of the way he mastered her body so completely, an orgasm began to unfurl.

"That's it." He thrust harder, leaving her gasping.

Closing her eyes, she came, screaming his name.

Still, relentlessly, he asked for more. When she was on the precipice once again, he pulled out.

She blinked, then looked up at him.

"I want you to put your legs over my shoulders."

That position would leave her helpless to the depth of his thrusts, but she nodded, placing her trust in him.

Quickly he adjusted their positions, and he moved himself closer, his shoulders pressing against the backs of her thighs.

It took her a few moments to get settled, and he braced himself on his palms, feasting his hungry gaze on her.

"I want you to keep your eyes open. I want you to see me, and I want to watch your responses."

She bit her lower lip as she nodded.

He took her again, stretching her wider than she'd ever been. Sex with him was more intense than anything she'd ever experienced. It wasn't just how big he was. It was how thoroughly he claimed her.

"You're my woman, Charlotte."

"Yes." In this moment, she was. The future, she refused to think about.

He thrust harder. Faster. Relentlessly. His eyes glazed over, and his arms trembled. She loved knowing this was every bit as powerful for him as it was for her.

His jaw tightened. "Charlotte…"

Moaning, she stroked his shoulder. She was lost, wanting him, wanting it.

"Mine."

After making sure she came once more, his eyebrows furrowed. "Fuck." He orgasmed, riding it, pulsing deep inside her.

She stayed in place, her body cradling his.

"Damn." He supported his upper body with one arm and traced a fingertip down her nose. "You're spectacular." His breathing ragged, he pulled back, then rolled onto his side to pull her against him. "I could have stayed in that position forever."

Her hamstrings would be tender for days. "It was a little physically demanding." Before he could respond, she placed a reassuring her hand on his chest. "That's not a complaint." In fact, she'd enjoyed it more than she would have imagined.

Even in a state of satiation, he had a leg on top of hers, protecting her.

Eventually he stirred, stroking hair away from her face. "That was… Are you okay?"

"I am." She nodded. "A little tender, I admit." The spanking with the vibrator had been mind-blowing, and she'd never tried that position before. "Honestly I've just never experienced anything like this before."

"Me either."

Did he mean that? Or was he being polite?

He left the bed to dispose of the condom, and he

returned with a warm washcloth. He bathed her pussy, soothing the tenderness. Though if his half-hard cock was any indication, his action might be a little self-serving. Impossibly, it appeared as though he might want to have sex again soon.

"Do you have any tiramisu left? I've been fantasizing about it."

She nodded. While she'd been thinking about him, he'd been thinking about her cooking? "Yes. Would you like me to get you some?"

"I can. Would you like some?"

"A huge slice. Seems I've worked up an appetite."

This was as fun as it was ridiculous. "We can go downstairs together." With a giggle, she hurried to the closet to grab a long silk robe while he pulled on his pants.

"You don't happen to own a pair of kitten slippers?"

"Open toed with heels?" She shook her head. "No."

"I'll buy you a pair."

Again he hinted at a future, one she wasn't foolish enough to allow herself to dream of.

Downstairs she pulled the pan from the refrigerator. "I have wine in the bar area over there." She pointed.

"Care for a glass?"

"You've got me spoiled already. I like bubbles with this. Just fair warning, I don't have any of the expensive stuff."

"Not needed."

While she served the dessert, he uncorked a bottle.

After grabbing some silverware and napkins, she glanced at him. "Where would you like to eat?"

"Any rules against the great room?"

"That sounds perfect."

He flipped the switch to turn on the fireplace, and they opted to sit together on the smallest sofa.

After taking his first bite of the tiramisu, he nodded

appreciatively. "Every bit as good as it was the other day. Maybe even better."

"Really?" She followed suit. "I wasn't sure how long it would last." He was right. The flavors had become more pronounced and the coffee-dipped lady fingers were still firm.

"You may have to show me how to make this."

"Do you actually cook?"

"No." He took another bite. "But I'd like to watch how you do it, and as a bonus I will get to eat the results."

She laughed. "You're impossible."

After they finished dessert, he took her plate, then offered her the champagne flute. Because it was natural, she curled up next to him, the ever-changing flames in the fireplace creating an easy intimacy. "Having you here... It's nice. The first time I've gotten to enjoy the space."

"Seems like somewhere you might want to spend time. Reading a book, watching television, or just relaxing."

She shrugged. "It was meant for a family. A gathering place."

"But your dad hasn't been up here, and your wedding was called off."

His words were gentle and considered, and unlike last time, they didn't sting as bad. Maybe she was moving on from the pain. "That's a nice way to put it."

"Does that mean you've sworn off relationships forever?"

"I haven't thought about it much." *Until now*. "Trust didn't come easy, and it was destroyed."

"Care to talk about it?"

She'd spent a lot of time avoiding that, pretending she was okay, smiling when people told her it was better she found out when she did. In retrospect, that was probably true, but hearing it while she was grieving had made her pain worse. With a falsely sunny smile, she'd internalized it all, locking it away in the tattered remnants of her heart. "I met Andy through mutual friends. He was wonderful, attentive. Had a great career as an attorney. We had a lot in common, and because he had a demanding schedule, he was understanding of the number of hours I put in. And the constant interruptions." Like Bradley calling and texting all weekend. "Even my dad liked Andy."

"That matters."

"It does." She took a small sip from her glass, then scooted around so that she could look at him more closely. "I couldn't be with someone he didn't approve of. Anyway…"

He waited.

"Andy did things the right way, asking my dad for permission to marry me. He proposed last Christmas when we were at my dad's house. You know, the whole romantic thing, in front of the tree, down on one knee. Everything was perfect."

"Except it wasn't."

She placed her glass on the coffee table. Maybe it was the fire or the wine or the awful memories, but she was suddenly warm. "A few months later my dad was working late." How could she say what happened next?

He waited.

"The punchline is that Dad caught Andy fucking my executive assistant. In my office."

"*Jesus*, Charlotte." Compassion radiated from his eyes, and his voice was jagged. "What a complete scumbag he was."

"It was humiliating."

"Not sure why." He placed his glass beside hers and took her hand in a reassuring grip. "His behavior was despicable. Treacherous. You did nothing wrong, and you have no need to feel embarrassed by his actions."

It wasn't that simple. "Everyone knew." Since then she'd buried herself in work and wore distrust like a coat of armor.

"That he screwed my admin made it worse. Julie and I were close. At least I thought. How well do we really know other people?"

He flinched just a little. "Indeed."

"That's really enough about me. How about you? It's kind of hard to believe you've never been in love."

He released her hand. "Seemed complicated."

Maybe a little like this?

"As a military family, we moved a lot. Saying goodbye to old friends and trying to make others... At some point it I recognized that any relationship I entered, I'd have to walk away from. With guys, it's one thing. But women... They're different. They're more tenderhearted. And it's difficult to move on."

"You sound a little like a hero. Sacrificing yourself for the greater good."

"Maybe I was trying to protect myself."

Interested, she tilted her head to one side.

"There was one girl my junior year in high school. Mindy Sue. Cheerleader. Straight-A student. We went to homecoming, but I knew nothing could come of it. Dad got transferred before the end of the first semester. After that..." He shrugged fatalistically. "Then I joined the military myself. Figured it was easier not to get involved. Lots of divorces among my friends."

"And now that you're out...?"

"I haven't thought about it much." He swept his gaze over her. "Maybe I could reconsider."

A delicious shiver rippled through her, and if sensing that, he leaned a little closer to her.

"The dessert was rich."

She nodded.

"Any ideas on how we should burn off the calories?"

"Yeah." She grinned. "Maybe one or two."

"Are you up for it? Not too sore?"

"I'm okay."

Desire flared in his eyes. "In that case…" He grabbed hold of her and reseated her on his lap, facing him. "Maybe you should finish what you started earlier."

"Maybe I should." Emboldened by his words and encouragement, she reached for the button at his waistband.

Garrett had never hated a mission like he did this one.

Protecting Charlotte Connelly? That was an honor. *But this…?*

Two hours ago he'd been paddling her delectable ass, and all of his attention was focused on pleasing her. Lovemaking had been mind-blowing. Her responses had been perfect, and their connection had been as physical as it was emotional.

Then they shared dessert and raw, honest conversation. As she shared the pain of her ex's betrayal, daggers had sunk into his heart. If the truth were told, what he was doing to her right now was no less despicable. And necessary.

Which was why he was in her office at two a.m., trying to access her computer to upgrade all of her security systems. While she slept—blissfully trusting him—he was violating her privacy.

It didn't matter that this was the right thing to do or that he was doing it at the request of her father who loved her, and he was paying the bill. Garrett still didn't like doing it.

Because this evening, things had become personal.

Goddamn it.

Earlier he'd told her the story about his high school love. Every word had been true, but he'd never shared that with anyone. Tonight, for the first time in his life, he was thinking about a future with a woman. Unfortunately it was a woman he couldn't have. When the thirty days were up, he would be reassigned, and he would never see her again.

"I've sent a temporary login to your phone, Commander Young."

The tech at the other end of the phone at Denver headquarters had no qualms about what he was doing, and Garrett was grateful. He needed to focus on the damn job, not let his thoughts be tormented by a beautiful woman he couldn't wait to get back to.

Garrett's device chimed.

The tech stayed on the line until Garrett was logged into the computer. "Let us know if there's anything else you need, Commander."

Five minutes later, soft sounds reached him. *Footsteps?* If so, that meant he didn't have time to get the cameras installed as Hawkeye had requested. Though they weren't the resolution of the ones she currently had, they were meant to fill in a couple of sightlines that had changed when she'd done some of the outdoor remodeling.

Focusing he finished what he was doing. Then he erased any trace that he'd been in her computer before logging out and putting it back into sleep mode.

Garrett comforted himself with the knowledge that she'd be better protected—even when he was no longer in her life.

He double-checked that he'd left everything as he'd found it before heading into the sunroom to stare out a window.

A light turned on behind him, and he turned to face the most beautiful woman he'd ever seen. She'd wrapped herself in a pink silk robe, and her hair was in beautiful disarray around her shoulders.

"I'm sorry." As he smiled, he swept his gaze over her, lingering, taking in every bit of her, memorizing each detail. "Did I disturb you?"

She cinched her belt a little tighter around her waist. "I often have trouble sleeping."

He remembered that from his discussion with Charlotte's former agent.

"Do you have insomnia too?"

"Typically? No. In the military, we learned to sleep when we could. Sitting up. Propped against a building even."

"I wish I knew what that was like." She tipped her head to the side. "So why are you up?"

"Do you want to know the truth?"

"I'm curious."

"My dick woke me up."

She laughed. "You can't be serious."

"Oh, I assure you I am." He grinned. "I didn't want you to be sore. So I let you sleep."

"Did you take care of yourself?"

Her question rocked him back on his heels. "No."

"You like to suffer?" A sensual gleam danced in her eyes as she glanced at the front of his pants.

His hard dick strained against the front of his pants. "It's heroic."

"I'd say." She closed the distance between them to slide her fingertips down his chest and to stroke his cock. "Are you ready to go back to bed?"

More than.

"Or would you like to stay up for a while? We have some wine left from earlier. Maybe soak in the hot tub."

"That's probably a good idea." That way she could soothe her body before he took her back to bed. "I don't have a swimsuit."

She grinned. "They're not allowed anyway."

"Now I'm even more interested."

"I think you'll enjoy it. If you want to take the lid off the hot tub, I'll grab the drinks."

"How about the code for the alarm? Not sure we want the sheriff showing up."

"Good idea." She crossed to a panel on the wall and typed in the code.

"You know Bonds has a whole-house computer. All you'd need to do is tell your version of Hello, Molly to unset the alarm."

"Isn't technology already intrusive enough?"

"Fair point. But I'm all about making things easier." Which might not be true. If he were serious about making her life less complicated, he would have kept his dick in his pants.

"Light switch is on the wall outside."

"Got it."

"I'll be right out."

The moment he opened the door, the below-freezing Colorado air seemed to suck oxygen from his lungs, and that galvanized him into action.

He removed the lid and placed it on the table.

As promised, she was right behind him. He took the plastic tumblers from her and placed them in the cup holders.

She opened a deck box and pulled out big, fluffy robes and enormous towels. "Can you put these over that chair so they don't get wet?"

"You've got this down to a science."

"Trial and error."

She reached back in for a ponytail holder and pulled her hair up before loosening the knot at her waist.

Transfixed, he stared at her.

As if aware of the power she held over him, she kept their gazes joined as she allowed the lapels to part. Then she shrugged so the silk could flutter to the ground.

Fuck me standing.

Her nipples hardened, and tiny goose bumps dotted her body, but she stood there like a goddess waiting for him to get naked.

He removed his boots and dropped his pants.

"Cold doesn't seem to have much effect on you, Mr. Young."

"It most certainly does." Since they'd made love, she seemed more relaxed, confident even. And he loved the transformation. "But your effect is stronger. Like the gravitational pull of the moon on the tides."

He offered his hand while she climbed the steps leading to the hot tub. Then she sank in to her chin.

As he entered she pushed a button to activate the jets and a second to turn on some soft lighting.

"I'll admit, this is deluxe." He sat close to her, then reached for one of the tumblers and offered it to her.

When they both had their drinks and were relaxed among the bubbles, they tapped their rims together.

"There's one in my condominium complex up here, but I'm not sure how management would react if I started using it naked."

She grinned. "I could see where that might be a problem."

Clouds drifted across the sky, hiding the stars.

Though his nose and ears were a little cool, the rising steam kept him warm enough.

"It's totally wonderful to do this when it snows."

"Is that an invitation."

She offered her tumbler back to him. "It might be."

For a few moments they said nothing, and instead just stared at the night sky.

The setting lent itself to romance, no matter how dangerous to his mission. "You mentioned you have trouble sleeping?"

"I'm not sure if that's the whole truth. I seem to wake up

thinking about a problem that I've been having at work. In the middle of the night with no ringing phones and no email interruptions, the answers come to me. As if I need peace in order for my mind to find solutions."

"The hour of writers, painters, poets?"

"Could be." She shrugged. "In a way it's sort of a habit now. Though I do like the magic of what you just said."

Clouds drifted apart, and a shooting star darted across the inky darkness.

"Make a wish." She closed her eyes.

He'd never believed in that kind of thing, but she made him want to. "What did you wish for."

"A trip."

"Anything special?"

"To see the aurora borealis. Maybe in a hotel with a glass roof where you lie in bed and get lost in the lights."

Garrett took a drink. He'd never thought much beyond the next job.

"How about you? Anything on your bucket list?"

"I have an antibucket list. Things I never want to see or experience again. War. Wounded children."

"I hate that for you."

"Sorry."

"Don't be. It's part of what makes you *you*."

Her tenderness might be his undoing.

But he hated to fuck up her evening with his moroseness. "If I did…"

She waited.

"There's a ski resort with a luge track. Parts of it appear vertical."

Her eyes widened. "You'd actually do that?"

"In a heartbeat."

"So you like adventure."

"Yeah, I do."

"Part of why you are into cryptocurrency? The risk involved?"

"It's different from jumping out of an airplane. But you've got a point. A different kind of thrill."

The jets shut off, and the bubbles settled.

"I recognize that look in your eyes."

"Do you? It's constant when you're near, Charlotte." He tucked damp, wayward strands of hair behind her ear, then leaned forward to give her a gentle kiss. "Shall we?"

He climbed out of the tub, then grabbed a towel for her.

"You're spoiling me."

Someone sure as hell should. And he fucking wanted it to be him.

As she snuggled into the warmth, he shucked water from his body, then dried off before grabbing their drinks and putting the lid back on the hot tub.

When they were inside, he followed her up the stairs.

"I like to shower after soaking. Get the chlorine off."

He joined her, soaping her body, then using the handheld unit to rinse her off.

"I mean it. I really am getting used to this."

So was he. "I want you on top this time." Where she'd have more control over the angle and the depth of his penetration.

When they were in bed, she sheathed his cock with a condom, each motion wonderful agony. But then she straddled him and lowered herself onto him, taking his dick a frustrating fraction of an inch at a time, and he realized that giving her control was easier in theory than it was in practice.

Concentrating on her, instead of himself, he dug his fingertips into her ass cheeks.

"Damn, Garrett!"

"Sore from your paddling?"

"That's…"

He hadn't left marks. This time. But he was glad to know the sensation lingered at least a little.

"Maybe next time we should use the wooden one."

"Yes, Sir."

A primal need to possess her rocked him. *Is there a sexier word in the English language?*

In a valiant effort to restrain himself, he moved one hand to cradle her breast. Then he squeezed into the soft flesh.

Tipping her head back, arching her back, she moaned. She was open for him, leaving herself completely exposed.

And he was done with waiting.

Seizing control, he pulled her toward him, capturing her mouth, plundering it simulating the fucking that he'd given her earlier.

Her breaths ragged, she pulled away to brace her hands on his chest. Then she sat up, taking him deep inside her, where he belonged.

Aching to orgasm but desperate to please her, he took hold of both of her nipples and twisted them slightly.

Charlotte thrashed wildly, crying out his name as she climaxed, her body clenching around him.

She was so damn hot. And it wasn't just her body. It was the way they'd connected emotionally.

Garrett was unable to last another moment. His balls drew up, and he came in hot spurts, pulling her against him, holding her there as if he'd never let her go.

"Mine." He meant it. He wasn't sure how, but she belonged with him—to him—and he would pay any price to make it happen. Unfortunately his lies loomed between them, and they grew larger every day.

CHAPTER NINE

HAWKEYE

"This isn't goodbye."

Charlotte drank in a steadying breath. What Garrett said made logical sense. But right now, her heart and brain were speaking different languages.

"This is 'see you soon.'" He shrugged, settling into his leather jacket.

"Of course." She gave him a brave smile.

Their time together last night had changed her. He'd coaxed responses from her that she hadn't known were possible.

And their conversation... Her trust in him ran deep. He listened intently, never prodding, but seeming to care about her answers. She'd told him things she'd never shared with another person.

Then this morning, the intimacy had continued.

He'd gotten up first and brewed a pot of coffee for them. They'd snuggled beneath the blankets as the caffeine had revitalized them, watching occasional wispy snowflakes float from the sky.

Then, happier than she'd been in years—or perhaps

happier than she'd ever been—she'd made brunch while he went for a short walk. When he returned, he helped with the meal, then insisted on doing all the cleanup.

"I mean it, Charlotte."

His booted footsteps loud on the hardwood floor, he closed the distance between them. His green eyes were narrowed intently as if he had nothing else to think about other than her.

Then he placed his thumb pad beneath her chin and tipped it back. "What we shared meant something."

How had he seen through her bravery and to the vulnerability she was so desperate to hide?'

"How about I take you to dinner tonight?"

Her heart fluttered. *Yes. A million times, yes.* If it was up to her heart, she'd seize every opportunity. Wrapped in the strength of his arms, she'd slept peacefully last night and for more hours than she had in months. It would be so easy to succumb to ridiculous flights of fancy, imagining a future with him.

And how stupid would that be?

She barely knew him. Being up here at the Steamboat ranch wasn't real life. She had a demanding job in town, and Garrett was a man who traveled a lot. He'd never mentioned that he was interested in settling down. In fact, he'd indicated the opposite. This was a thirty-day fling. Not forever.

Besides, because they'd spent so much time together and it was already close to two o'clock and her call with Bradley, she had half a dozen things still on her checklist, including checking in on her dad and all of her weekend chores.

As much as she wanted to go to dinner and then see where the evening led, she couldn't afford the time away.

And yet... If this was a fling, she wanted to savor every moment. If he didn't sleep over, she could stay up late to catch up. "I'd love that."

A smile sauntered across his lips, making her tummy do a somersault.

"I'll make reservations."

"Reservations?" Which meant he was planning something nice.

"Wear something sexy." He leaned down just a little closer, stealing the air she was going to breathe. "The truth is you could wear anything at all, and I would think you were the most beautiful woman in the world." He traced her cheek. "Think of me."

Then leaned in closer to seal her lips with his in a way that guaranteed she would think of nothing but him.

When he had her pulse racing and her body on fire, he ended the kiss. *Damn you.* It took the barest of touches for her to be ready for him.

"I'll pick you up at six."

Nodding, she followed him to the door to key in the code to turn off the alarm. Already he had her remembering to set it.

"You know there's an app for that."

She returned his smile.

"My mother said I always have to make sure a woman is safe and taken care of."

"How can I argue with your mom? I promise I will set it when you leave."

When he studied her, as if trying to be certain, she made a tiny X on her chest.

He nodded with satisfaction before opening the door. On the porch, he stopped and turned back to her, capturing her face in his palms and kissing her until she had to reach for the wall for stability.

"Damn. I don't want to leave."

That's two of us.

"I'm going while I still can." Once he released her, he pivoted to jog down the few steps to his car.

He gave her a quick wave before climbing behind the wheel.

As was becoming a habit, she watched him until the car vanished. Then, keeping her promise, she locked up after him and reset the alarm.

Trying her best to refocus, she checked her watch. She had about fifteen minutes until her meeting with Bradley, which gave her just enough time to brew a cup of chamomile tea.

When she was halfway to the kitchen, her phone rang.

Since it could be her father, she crossed to her office to check caller ID.

Bradley. She sighed. He couldn't wait for their appointment?

Since she wasn't quite ready to deal with him yet, she sent him to voicemail. The tiny act of rebellion was more satisfying than she could have imagined.

Twenty minutes later, beverage in hand, she answered his third call.

"Bradley."

"Jesus, Char."

She imagined him dragging his hand through his hair in frustration.

"I've been worried. Where have you been?"

"Cooking. Enjoying my day off." She took a sip of the soothing drink. "I highly recommend it."

"It's bad enough that you've taken a month off, but—"

"Bradley, that's not exactly—"

"Now you're not answering your phone either. You're the owner's daughter. Everyone watches what you do. You have to set a good example for the rest of the employees."

After the evening she had with Garrett, she wasn't in the

mood to engage with Bradley. The sooner she wrapped up this call, the better. That way she'd get through her to-do list and still have a chance to take a hot bath, something her body needed.

The thought made her grin.

"Are you listening?"

"Of course." She took a breath. "Before we move on, taking Sunday off is something I highly recommend for all our employees. Even you."

"Malcolm expects our report by the end of the year."

"So why are you wasting our valuable time? I've only penciled in thirty minutes for this call."

"What the hell is going on there, Char? You're not yourself."

Maybe she was. More so than ever.

She glanced at the clock. "Twenty-four minutes left."

"I think you need to come home."

"If that's the purpose of this discussion, we can hang up and get back to our lives."

"You need to take this succession plan seriously."

Instead of responding, she sipped her tea. Maybe she should have made a pot instead of a cup. "You said you have some ideas. I'm listening."

But instead of remaining at her desk, she stood and walked to the sunroom. Every place in her house now contained memories of Garrett, and she took comfort from that.

She curled up on a couch overlooking the patio.

"Can I speak frankly?"

"Please do."

"We both know that you don't want to be the eventual owner *and* CEO."

True. That was no secret.

"But your father will expect to see that in our plan."

"Agree." There was no way someone unrelated to the first Connelly would be allowed to inherit the company. Nor would her father allow it to be broken apart and sold off.

"For the last few years, I've been his right-hand man. I'm the logical choice to be CEO."

No doubt he'd do an excellent job, and she shared her father's appreciation of Bradley's talent, hard work, dedication, and ambition.

"Do you agree?"

"Yes."

"We can do great things together."

"It won't be for a long time. Many years."

"Your father may begin turning over some responsibilities. That's the only thing that makes sense and why he's pushing so hard."

"He'll still be in the ownership seat." She had to admit, having this settled would make sense, and it may take some pressure off her. And no doubt that was what her father was hoping she'd see. If he wasn't running day-to-day operations, he may even have more time to pursue new opportunities which would make him happier.

"There's only one way this could be more perfect."

"I'm listening."

For a moment, he didn't answer. Then he took a deep breath. "We need to get married."

"What?" She put down her cup so the remnants of her tea didn't slosh over the rim. "Are you out of your mind?"

"I have given this a lot of thought. Once you've had time to consider the options, I think you'll agree this is the only thing that makes sense."

Her mind reeled as she tried to keep up with what he was saying.

"The company's future will be secured. Our children will be the heirs to your family legacy."

Children?

"We get along well, and we both want what's best for Connelly. You can be certain your father will give his blessing." He fell silent for a moment. "I would be loyal and true to you."

Clearly he wasn't above weaponizing the horrible memory of what had happened with Andy.

"I'm sure you'd like to do this the right way. We can announce our engagement over the Christmas holidays. We can get married next summer. People might be surprised, but they certainly won't be shocked."

"Bradley." He'd been desperate to talk to her because he'd been planning their wedding? "Stop."

"I've been shopping for rings, and I can send a few over to you for your opinion before I make the final purchase. Unless there's an heirloom you'd prefer to use."

"*Stop.*"

"This is the satisfactory plan that your father has been looking for."

From his point of view, a marriage of convenience made complete sense. Maybe she would have considered it. Until Garrett.

"We can discuss it when you're back in town. Unless you'd like me to come up there to talk about it in person?"

"No." She definitely did not want to share this place with Bradley. "I appreciate how forward thinking you've been, but I assure you that marriage will not be part of the plan." Before he could interrupt again, she finished. "Is there anything else you wanted to discuss?"

"Us getting married is the only thing that makes sense. It will ensure Connolly and Company's success long into the future."

"If there's nothing else, my father is expecting to hear

from me." Yet another half-lie. Anything to put an end to this conversation.

"I think he'll like my proposal."

She scowled. Had Bradley already talked to her dad? "Enjoy the rest of your weekend." Without waiting for a response, she pressed the End button and stared at her screen.

Restless energy churning in her, she stood to pace the room as she called her dad.

The phone rang several times, long enough that she wondered if he was going to answer. When he did, his voice was gruff.

"I'm sorry. Did I catch you napping?"

"Watching a football game." The noise in the background vanished.

"Who's winning?"

"Not our team."

Which was why she rarely watched. "I just got off the phone with Bradley."

"Did you?" His tone was more curious than anything.

"He thinks we should get married."

"Oh?" Malcolm was noncommittal. If he knew anything, he was playing it cool.

"He says it will be the perfect answer to your succession plan. In time, I would become owner, and he could be CEO of the holding company."

"Interesting idea."

"And then our children will become the Connelly heirs."

"What did you say to his proposal?"

Instead of answering, she countered with a question of her own. On so many levels, it was a logical choice. "Did you know anything about this?"

"Something Bradley came up with all on his own. Though if it made you happy I would not be averse to it."

"So this wasn't a plan that the two of you concocted?"

"My precious Charlotte. Nothing is more important to me than you are. I cherish your happiness above all things. Would I love to have grandchildren to spoil? Absolutely. You know your mom and I planned on having a house full of kids."

Until now, she'd been unable to imagine a love as deep as theirs. Almost two decades had passed, and her dad still had a hole in his heart that no one else could fill.

Yet Garrett had that effect on her.

If he hadn't shown up in her life when he did, would she have agreed to Bradley's suggestion? Since Andy, she'd avoided relationships. But the idea of a loving husband and children was still out there...

But when she imagined her future, it wasn't Bradley she saw there. It was Garrett.

"Do you think I'm trying to get you married off so I can have grandkids?"

The ridiculousness of his question reassured her.

"And am I correct in assuming your answer was no?"

"Bradley is a good person. He works as hard as anyone I know." Maybe too much even. "But he's not for me."

"The heart knows what it wants."

Charlotte came to a stop near the window. As always the landscape soothed. "Yes." *It does.*

With that behind them, she turned back to business. "Any update on Workflow.ai?"

"Still looking into their financials. Hired an investigator."

"That's serious."

"Why hide the members of an LLC?"

"Could be Workflow doesn't know? I can understand getting an investment from an LLC and not knowing all the members involved." She shrugged. "On the other hand, no one understands business the way you do. You're smart to look into it." She paused before delicately asking her next question. "How are you feeling?"

"I'll be better when I can get back to my football game." As if to punctuate his statement, noise filled the background.

Evidently he'd unmuted the television.

"I can take a hint."

"That wasn't a hint." He laughed. "Enjoy what little remains of your weekend. Before Bradley calls again."

"I'll talk to you tomorrow."

Since she still had a little time before she needed to get ready for her date with Garrett—something she was ridiculously excited for—Charlotte returned to her office to clean out her email inbox.

The first was from the head of IT advising of downtime to upgrade security systems. Another was from HR with the weekly job postings and recommendations for next year's cost of living increases.

Those handled, she moved on to requests from the accounting department. Costs of new Bonds computers had gone up. No surprise there. And they needed to purchase ten for remote workers, putting them over budget. Since it was necessary, she approved the expenditure.

Then she opened the next one.

Hey, Charlotte.

This month's bill from Hawkeye Security is more than ten percent higher than last month's. Okay to pay?

~Jayne

Curious, she clicked on the attachment, and her entire world shattered around her.

CHAPTER TEN

HAWKEYE

Garrett's phone vibrated.

Since he was pedaling the exercise bike furiously, he considered ignoring the summons. Instead he grabbed the device to check the caller ID.

Charlotte.

His pulse, already near max heart rate, accelerated.

She was the only person he'd interrupt his workout for. Slowing he smiled and answered. "I'm looking forward to seeing you tonight."

"Is it possible for you to come early?"

"Yeah." The more time with her, the better. Since they'd been apart, his thoughts had been consumed with her. He'd never been obsessed with a woman like he had with her. She wasn't a job to him. She was someone he could picture a future with. "Is everything okay?"

"Something we need to discuss."

Now that he wasn't breathing as hard, he tuned into the nuance in her tone. There was a brittle edge to it that he hadn't heard before. "What time do you want me there?"

"As soon as possible."

He scowled. "You sure everything is okay?"

"It's fine." But her voice was stretched thin.

"You're making me nervous."

She said nothing.

"Are you in danger?"

"Not in the way you mean."

He knew his lover and her moods. "Hang on. I'll be there as quick as I can."

His next call was to the surveillance team who reported no activity at the ranch. Then he checked in with Torin and Mira to let them know his plans.

In record time he'd showered, changed, and then headed to the ranch house.

The drive lasted forever, and he edged past the speed limit every chance he got. When he stopped at the entrance to her property and pushed the call button, she didn't respond.

Getting worried, he called her.

Though she didn't pick up, the gates parted.

He took the curves too fast, and for the first time she wasn't waiting for him in the open doorway.

What the fuck is going on? Whatever it was, he didn't like it.

He tested the knob to discover the door was locked. At least that was a step in the right direction.

He rang the bell and waited. Then he waited some more.

Finally she answered.

Her hair was pulled back from her face in a ponytail. Her features were stark, and her eyes glassy. As if she'd been crying.

Garrett frowned. "What's wrong?"

As he reached to touch her, she held up a hand to keep him at a distance.

"Don't! Don't touch me."

For the first time in his life, he was at a total loss. He was standing within two feet of the woman who meant more to him than any woman ever had, but a massive gulf stretched between them, one he didn't know how to bridge. "What do you need, baby?"

"Don't call me that."

"Okay." His heart thumped in a rapid-fire beat. He looked beyond her to assess any imminent threat and saw none. Something with her father, maybe? He took a breath, drawing on his resources to stay calm and sharp.

"There's something I'd like you to see."

Her no-nonsense heels clicked out a threatening tattoo on the floor, and adrenaline lay curled in his stomach as he followed her to her office.

She took her place behind her desk. At once she was a commanding, formidable executive. "Have a seat."

"Look, Charlotte..." He dug his hand into his hair. "I'm not sure—"

"I said have a seat, Mr. Young." She waited until he complied before continuing. "If that's your real name."

The fuck? His word tilted as she tapped her finger on top of a file folder.

Then, never taking her gaze off him, she slid it across the desk. "Go ahead and open it."

Scowling, trying to keep one eye on her, he flipped open the folder. *Fuck. Fucking fuck.* He didn't need to see past the first page to know the entire mission had been compromised.

"Care to explain?"

"Charlotte..." He closed the folder and dragged his hand through his hair. "It's not what you think."

"Of course it's not." Her smile was as fake as it was fragile. "So how about you tell me what parts I have wrong." Without giving him any opportunity to respond, she went on. "You don't work for Hawkeye?" Again, she continued. "Or Operation Snowfall doesn't exist? Or Snow Queen is only in my imagination? I suppose it's better than Ice Princess."

"Jesus, Charlotte—" He waved his hand impatiently. "All that is correct. But it doesn't tell the whole story."

"Which is? That you got paid to fuck me?"

Her words were a dagger. Furious, insulted, hurting for her, he came to his feet and placed his hands on her desk, leaning toward her. *"Stop."*

If he didn't know her so well, he might not have noticed the way her shoulders went rigid, and her breaths turned shallow. She was spiraling and needed him more now than ever.

Yet the emotional wall she'd built between them was one he didn't know how to demolish.

"I can't believe I was so stupid as to believe your lies. All of them." Her voice broke and took his heart along with it. "I trusted you."

"Don't, Charlotte. Don't." Frantically he shook his head. "This may have started as a job, but we both know it's not that. Not anymore."

"Everything's a lie, isn't it?" She choked on a sob as if she was barely holding on to her emotions.

"You've told me the parts that are a lie, but I'll tell you the parts that weren't. What we shared in bed, that was real. I..." Damn it. This wasn't the way he imagined it. "I love you."

"How fucking dare you?"

"Charlotte."

"I've heard enough from you, Garrett. It is Garrett, isn't it?"

"And my middle name is Christopher. Everything about my military service is true."

"Your mom?"

He winced. "She abandoned me and my dad when I was a baby."

"So you grew up without a mother? Maybe that explains why you're so damn heartless."

She'd already sunk her dagger, and now she twisted it.

Helpless, he dropped his shields, allowing her to glimpse his own pain. "There's nothing heartless about what I feel for you."

"Let me make this clear." She brought up her chin and met his gaze. "You're fired. Not only are you fired, but so is all of Hawkeye. There are other security firms out there with your resources who I'm sure would be glad to earn our business while behaving more ethically."

The woman knew how to wield words as weapons.

No doubt Hawkeye could be replaced, but the integration of personal protection and physical buildings security, along with IT solutions across the holding company and all subsidiaries, would take months to get in place. In the meantime she would be vulnerable. And that bothered him more than anything.

"I'll let Hawkeye know that this ridiculous scheme has cost them millions of dollars a year."

"As if I give a single damn about Hawkeye at this moment. You're the only thing that matters. I understand you're hurt, and I own my part of that. And I apologize from the bottom of my heart." He kept her gaze hostage and dropped all of his emotional shields. He wanted—needed—her to see the truth, the devastation in his eyes. "The moment we met, this stopped being a job to me. And I will tell you this—"

"You need to leave."

He absolutely would honor her wishes even if it destroyed him. He swallowed the jagged edges of anguish that ripped into his heart. "You will find another security company. But no one—no one—will ever protect you like I would. You own a part of my soul, Charlotte."

"Then maybe you shouldn't have fucked me." She blinked

back her tears. "You're a bastard, Garrett Young. See yourself out." With that, she stood.

Motions calm and methodical, never looking back, she left the room. Tracking her motions, he turned to watch her climb the stairs.

A door sealed with a decisive click. Then fainter, but still discernible across the distance, a snick drifted on the air as she turned a lock, closing him out of her life.

As if he knew he was being watched, Garrett paused before getting in his vehicle and looked up at the window where she was watching him.

For at least a minute—a moment and eternity wrapped into one—he stood there, his features gaunt. His emotions appeared real, just like they had in her office, just like they had that first night when he'd slipped into the gondola behind her. And if she hadn't known the truth, she might have fallen for his smiling lies once again.

What an idiot she was, believing the fantasy he'd created.

The truth was, his charade would have ended anyway, the moment she returned to Denver.

He would have vanished from her life as if their time together hadn't happened and didn't matter.

Better now than later.

At least that's what she tried to tell the tattered remnants of her heart.

Downstairs her phone rang once, then twice. She ignored it in favor of seeing Garrett drive out of her life for the last time.

Her phone repeated its incessant urgings for an hour, maybe more.

But then reality intruded.

Her whole life, she'd dealt with unpleasantries straight on.

In firing him and Hawkeye Security, she'd dropped a bomb that would have repercussions throughout the organization. No doubt her father had heard about it.

She wouldn't absolve him of responsibility either. He was the one who'd set everything in motion, making her a pawn in his very real and very emotionally devastating game of chess.

After splashing cold water on her face, she returned downstairs. She pretended not to notice that this was about the time that Garrett would have been arriving to take her to a very special dinner that preceded a spectacular night.

Resolutely she swallowed the knot of grief lodged in her throat, then made her way to her office to pick up her cell phone.

27 missed calls.

Most of them were from her father. A handful were from Hawkeye Security. And of course, two had come from Bradley. *Ironic.* This afternoon, she'd fantasized that love was more important than practicality.

She curled up into the corner of the too-big, too-lonely couch where Garrett had spanked her, held her, protected her.

Shaking her head to clear it, she dialed her father.

"God, Charlotte. I was starting to get worried."

"Just another day of being betrayed by the people I care about."

He was silent as her words quietly found their mark.

"What were you thinking, Dad?" Did he have any idea what he'd done?

"I love you and wouldn't survive if anything happened to you."

"You could have talked to me."

"I have. I did." He exhaled his exasperation. "After Aubrey left, you refused to even consider protection."

She winced, remembering that she'd called her former agent and asked her to check out Garrett. Aubrey, too, had been in on this entire conspiracy. Where did it fucking end? "You've obviously heard that I fired Hawkeye."

"Yeah. And I understand your anger. They were just trying to please their client."

"Perhaps it escaped everyone's notice that I am the client also."

"No one is debating that, Charlotte."

Now that she'd vented her frustration, she noticed a strain in his voice.

"I worry about you."

"Dad." She sighed. *How many times have we had this conversation?* "I'm a grown-up."

He was silent for a very long time. "We should talk."

She frowned. "That's what we're doing right now."

"In person."

Alarm flooded her. "I'll have my admin charter a flight."

"No need to panic. It can wait for tomorrow."

Which would leave her on these hundreds of acres alone with her memories and heartbreak. She'd rather take action. And right now, nothing was more important than being with her father. "I'll see you soon."

After placing the phone call, she packed her essentials, then headed out to her car. When she turned on to the main road, a vehicle pulled off the shoulder and slid in behind her.

Hawkeye? Or someone else?

Glancing constantly in the rearview mirror, she used voice activation to dial her emergency contact at Hawkeye. "There's a vehicle following me."

"Please stand by for a moment, Ms. Connelly."

Her knuckles whitened on the steering wheel as she continued her drive toward the airport.

The woman, with her reassuring voice, came back on the line. "They're Hawkeye operatives, ma'am."

"Even though I fired your company?"

"I apologize, Ms. Connelly. That's above my paygrade. Would you like me to transfer your call?"

"Thank you. I'll handle it myself."

"Please let me know if there's anything else I can do for you."

With a quick thanks, Charlotte pushed the End button on her screen.

Within minutes, she was in the parking lot with her shadow off to the side. When she exited her vehicle, so did a woman.

Mira Araceli.

Charlotte sighed.

Was everyone part of this circus?

Computer backpack slung over her shoulders and carrying a small bag, she climbed the steps into the aircraft and was soon on her way home.

Though she tried to work, her mind raced a million different directions. But when she reclined her seat and tried to rest, memories of Garrett swarmed back in—tiny snippets of conversation, or the lingering memory of his touch and lazy explorations of her body, and her own moments of ecstasy.

A seemingly endless amount of time later, she was on the tarmac in Denver.

Her usual driver was waiting for her.

"Evening, Saul."

"Welcome home, Ms. Connelly. Where to?"

"My dad's, please."

With a sharp nod, he closed her into the back seat and then joined the light Sunday evening traffic.

After she sent a text to her father saying she was on her way, she leaned forward. "Saul?"

"Ma'am?" In the rearview mirror, he met her gaze.

"Do you work for Hawkeye?"

When he didn't immediately respond, she sighed. "You too, huh?"

So this man who had been with her for years would be out of a job. Damn it. There were other security companies out there that were the same size as Hawkeye, but she had a personal relationship with Saul. Two months ago he and his beautiful wife, Cassie, had welcomed their second baby.

She tightened her ponytail. Why did this have to be so complicated?

He turned on some light jazz, not making conversation as he drove toward her father's house in Cherry Creek. That had been another of her mom's purchases. She'd loved the vibrant area and had bought a small place during a market downturn.

The home she'd built was now worth a small fortune. Another one of her brilliant strategic moves. That thought led her right back to Garrett and his stories—*lies*—about the mother he'd never known. He spoke of her as if she'd existed. Despite herself, Charlotte thought about the young boy he might have been. Had he had the same impish smile? What emptiness had he endured? Even though she'd lost her mother, Charlotte had known her love. What must it have been like to grow up without a mom's comfort and with only a hardened military officer to guide him?

Had it truly made him heartless?

She tried to shove the question aside. But when he'd leaned over her desk earlier, there'd been rawness and vulnerability in the depth of his startling green eyes. He'd told her he loved her, but that couldn't possibly be true. And even if it was, it didn't matter. She couldn't be with someone who lied to her.

A few minutes later, Saul parked in her father's driveway.

"Thank you. I know you need to get back to Cassie and the baby, so I'll take one of Dad's cars home tonight."

"If it's just the same to you, ma'am, my shift ends at midnight."

"In that case, thank you." She exited the car, then used a code to let herself into her dad's house.

He met her in the foyer. Though he was dressed as she expected in trousers and a dress shirt, he looked thinner than he had even ten days ago.

She narrowed her gaze but accepted the hug he offered. "Do you want to tell me what's going on, Dad?"

"Join me in my study." Once there, he poured himself a whiskey.

Memories were everywhere, captured by a camera lens. There was a formal portrait from the day he married her mom, a snapshot of them as a family on vacation in Steamboat, one of her in ski school, her high school senior picture, yet another from her college graduation.

"Can I get you a glass of wine?"

"No. Thanks." But she snagged a bottle of water from the top of his makeshift bar and sat across from him as she'd done hundreds of times through the years.

All of their important conversations had happened in this room, from discussing her grades, to boyfriend issues, budgets for her prom gowns, then ultimately school majors, then plans for her to join Connelly and Company. Most recently she'd avoided the topic of succession planning. "What's going on, Dad?"

"I wanted this to wait until you were back from your month away."

She put her unopened bottle on a coaster.

"I'm okay."

Her mind reeled. Any conversation that began that way didn't have a happy ending.

"It appears I may have had a minor heart attack."

He continued, but she couldn't make sense of the words as the world collapsed around her for a second time that day.

"Things are under control... No need to worry. I'm in good hands... I intend to live a long, long time..."

"Dad." She couldn't catch her breath. She was a strong person, but she wasn't sure how much she really could endure. "Appears? May have? Or did?"

"It was minor. But it explains why I've been tired."

A sob catching in her throat, she rushed to him. He stood and gathered her against him, comforting her, stroking her hair, though she was the one who should have been there for him.

"I had no idea. Why didn't you tell me?"

"Because I'm okay." When they ended their embrace, he held her shoulders. "I've got a prescription, and I'm getting medical care."

"But..."

"There's nothing else to do. I'm going to work fewer hours, spend time in nature more. Enjoy life. Like you should be right now."

Instead of pulling away, she remained where she was.

"According to Dr. Van, there's no reason I can't live to a hundred."

She managed the small smile as he'd intended. "Promise?"

"I've got a lot to live for, Charlotte."

A few minutes later they resumed their seats.

"We need to be practical. I can't let any rumors about my health get out."

Of course. Practicalities.

"It would affect the business, maybe the profitability of the subsidiaries."

Trying to keep up with his thoughts, she exhaled. This was new for her, but he'd had time to process and decide on a plan.

"You're an heiress, Charlotte. And if anything were to hit the press…" He rolled his glass between his palms but didn't take a drink. "The threat to you is real."

"I wish you had come to me."

"And if I had?" He regarded her. "You would have fretted. There was nothing you could do here or for me. I wanted you to have your month away."

"You mean more to me than any trip to Steamboat."

"I appreciate that." He smiled. "Put yourself in my shoes. Wouldn't you want your child to enjoy her life fully? To do the things she loves?"

"That's not fair."

"Life has taught me that."

It had. With the passing of his own father when he was so young and the loss of his wife. "But you shouldn't have had to shoulder this burden alone." And no wonder he was focused on the succession plan. He needed everything lined up.

"Knowing you're safe is the only thing that allows me to sleep at night."

She gave a lopsided grin. "Is this your way of asking me not to fire Hawkeye?"

"You run day-to-day ops at Connelly and Company. If that's your decision, I will abide by it."

His words hung in the air, unfinished.

"But?" she prompted.

"Their contract has a kill fee of a million dollars."

"Damn." She winced. "That's significant."

"Or you could start talking to new firms and then just not

renew their contract next year." He moved the glass to the side.

That made sense. It would take months to get another firm in place.

"The truth is, the blame belongs on me, not Hawkeye. I understand you're furious with me. Rightfully so. I'll accept that."

Knowing what she knew, how could she blame him?

"All that said, if there was dereliction of duty on their part, we have an escape clause we can potentially use. You'd have to consult legal."

"Dereliction? No."

"Then what was it?"

For as long as she could remember, she'd told her father everything. But this was too personal. "My bodyguard..." Is that what he was? Nothing more?

"Garrett Young?"

"Do you know him?"

"He was headed for Cozumel when Hawkeye called him. Out of all the protective agents in the Denver area, I requested him." He leveled a knowing glance at her. "Did I screw up?"

"No. Not you." *Me.* "Things got"—Charlotte searched for the word—"Personal."

"Do you want to talk about it?"

She shook her head.

"Those types of relationships can be complicated."

"Dad. I didn't know who he was. And..." *And...*

"You fell for him?"

She lanced her palms with her fingernails. "I let him get too close." After Andy she should have known better.

"You're hurt."

Her father knew her too well for her to pretend otherwise.

"That means he meant something to you."

Maybe too much.

"If it has any bearing on your decision making, he's no longer with Hawkeye."

Why did the news matter to her?

"He resigned. Accepted full responsibility for the failure of the mission." Malcolm shrugged. "Rightly so. Saved Hawkeye the inevitability of firing him." He pushed back his chair and stood. "It's been a long day, Charlotte. Go home. Get some rest. Then go back to Steamboat."

"You know I can't do that." She could sort out the logistics tomorrow. Have the caretaker close up the house and get her car from the airport parking lot. "I'll stay here with you."

He bristled. "Absolutely not. I don't want you underfoot."

She scowled.

"I will see you at the office tomorrow."

"Dad—"

"Either go back to Steamboat, Charlotte, or I'll see you at the office in the morning." With that he headed for the front door.

In the foyer she tipped her head to the side uncertainly. "Are you sure?"

"Good night, my precious daughter."

Not wanting to leave but having no choice, she walked outside to find Saul waiting for her with the back door open. "Did you know? About my dad's health?"

"Mr. Connolly swore me to secrecy, ma'am."

She nodded, appreciating his loyalty. "I understand and appreciate you for waiting."

"It's not always just about duty, ma'am. I wanted to be sure you were okay."

That he'd known and cared about her, not just as a client but as a person, meant the world to her. "I can't thank you enough."

"Anytime, ma'am." In silence he drove her home, then bid her good evening.

Inside her downtown condominium, lost and alone in a way she'd never been before, she stood in the dark, staring into the abyss of uncertainty that was her future.

Now that her heart was shattered, what the hell step was she supposed to take next?

CHAPTER ELEVEN

HAWKEYE

"You look like shit."

Garrett turned his head to see his old army buddy Kane standing next to him. "Nice to see you too, asshole."

"Mind if I join you?"

Without waiting for an answer, Kane slid onto the barstool next to Garrett. Garrett picked up his bottle and angled it to his friend in acknowledgment. He didn't bother asking how Kane found him. The Muddy Duck was a designated AMM. After Mission Meetup. For years, ever since their military days, they'd had one. In fact, they'd had an AMM even when they were active duty.

And he didn't bother asking why Kane was here at two o'clock on a Wednesday afternoon. No doubt he'd heard Garrett was *no longer with* Hawkeye.

"What're you drinkin'?" The bartender placed a coaster in front of Kane. Since there were few other customers, service was great.

"Same as my friend here."

A moment later, a low-carb light beer was set in front of

Kane, and he winced. "Since it's open, it's too late to change my order?"

Garrett shrugged. "Lime helps."

"Guess I'll get my vitamin C if nothing else."

The bartender brought over a small plastic cup filled with seen-better-day fruit quarters.

"Figured you'd be headed to Cozumel."

The rest of Kane's sentence hung in the stale air, unfinished. *Now that you don't have anything else to do.* "Things change."

"Yeah, man. They do." Kane force-fed three pieces of lime into the neck of the bottle.

Garrett shook his head. "You should have ordered one of your fancy-shmancy microbrews."

"They don't have them here."

Which was another reason this was his favorite AMM.

Garrett lifted his beer and took a long drink, staring into the mirror behind the bar. Did he look like shit? Unshaven, yes. But he was still working out and showering.

"When's the last time you slept?"

For more than an hour or two at a time? Last Saturday night. In Charlotte's bed.

"Might not be a bad thing for you to get away, man. Get some distance."

Garrett didn't want to discuss what happened. Didn't want company. But Kane was a persistent sonofabitch, and Garrett he had no secrets from his brother-in-arms.

They'd both done things they weren't proud of, things that haunted them in the middle of the night, things they didn't talk about. But the shit that preyed on Kane was the stuff of nightmares. "I fucked up."

"We all do."

"Crossed a line. She said I had no integrity." That still rattled him. "She's right."

"That's horseshit."

Garrett appreciated his friend's loyalty. "I let it get personal. Didn't cross the lines—I fucking obliterated them." Too late he realized the rules didn't just exist for the client's safety. They existed for the agent's as well.

He'd fucked his career. But in the scope of things, that was of little consequence. It was the damage he'd done to Charlotte—the betrayal in her eyes—that he would carry to his grave.

"What are you going to do for work?"

He took another drink, then grinned. "Thought maybe I'd look into cryptocurrency." For the immediate future, he had enough money that he wasn't worried about paying the bills. Long enough, at any rate, to get his fucking head on straight, which it wasn't right now.

Kane was right. So was Hawkeye. Even Inamorata. Garrett should go someplace that didn't have memories of Charlotte.

The damnedest thing was, he couldn't walk away even though common sense insisted he haul his scuba gear to the airport and get on a plane.

Kane fell silent, looking up at the television that was playing highlights from last weekend's ballgames, giving Garrett time to talk at his own pace.

The bartender passed by, and Kane raised his finger to capture her attention. "I want to trade this in on a soda."

Garrett blinked. "The fuck?"

"Figured if you're not drinking beer, I won't either." He slid the still-full bottle as far away as he could. "We need a new AMM if you're going to be morose. Somewhere we can both get drunk."

"Still on my first."

"Great. So it sucks *and* it's warm. You're not doing the *I got my ass fired so I'm drowning my sorrows* act with any conviction."

Garrett snickered. "Yeah."

"Fuck, Young." Kane angled his head so he could get a better look at Garrett. "You're not done with the mission."

When Garrett didn't respond, Kane swore again. "Fuck."

He should walk away. Needed to. Had been instructed to—in no uncertain terms.

After the confrontation in Charlotte's office, he'd informed the team he needed a meeting. Then he dialed Hawkeye.

At the Walker Ranch, he'd been transparent about what happened and the fact he was turning in his resignation.

Everyone was quiet, thoughtful, except for Elissa who was worried about the effects on Charlotte. Jacob's intended had warned Garrett from the beginning. But he'd ignored that as well as all the other danger signs that had flashed in front of him.

They'd looked at the logistics. Even though Charlotte had fired Garrett, and the entire security firm, the contract was still in force until they heard otherwise.

But Hawkeye had been clear. Garrett was off the mission. The new commander was Torin Carter, and Garrett needed to leave the meeting. And as of the next morning, he would no longer have use of the rental condominium. Adding insult to injury, he had to find his own way back to Denver. Not that he minded; the drive would help clear his mind.

Jacob and Torin walked him to the door, and the fucking cat hissed at him, baring her teeth as if she too knew he'd blown the operation.

Before walking away, he met Torin's eyes. "Keep her safe."

"You have my word."

The door shut behind him, and he stood still, shocked, broken.

In that moment he lost everything that had ever mattered to him. His team. Camaraderie. The woman he loved.

Numb, Garrett spent the night feeling damn sorry for himself, mourning his losses.

But the next day, following a punishing workout, he'd vowed not to take no for an answer.

He placed a phone call that took a lot of courage and a shitpile of balls. In returning, he'd accepted the verbal lashing he deserved.

And then he'd returned to Denver.

"Do I even want to know what the hell you're doing?" Kane's question cut through Garrett's ruminations.

"No."

Kane clapped Garrett on the back. *"I hope you know what you're doing, man."*

So did he. But what the hell was he supposed to do from here?

He sipped his too-warm beer.

There was nothing else for him to lose.

THE NUMBER ON HER CALLER IDENTIFICATION SCREEN MADE Charlotte blink.

Elissa Conroy. No doubt she was deep into her wedding plans.

Charlotte was on the way from the accounting office and back to her own, and she paused in the hallway, her momentary smile fading.

It wasn't just a wedding. It was an event she was no longer planning to attend.

The thought sent a little pang through her heart. Not just because she wouldn't be joining them for the celebration, but because her life had become so entwined with Garrett's, despite the little time they spent together.

It still didn't make sense to her.

How had she fallen in love so quickly?

And why did his absence still ache so deeply?

Her insomnia was worse than ever, and every day she brought baked goods into the office, even though there were still plenty of treats leftover from the day before. It wasn't just her father's health that bothered her, it was the torturous thought about Garrett and the future that would never be.

Before the call went to voicemail, she swiped to answer and continued toward her office.

"Charlotte." Genuine warmth rang from Elissa's voice. "I'm so glad I caught you."

"I'm surprised you even have time to think."

"It's been crazy." Elissa laughed. "I've been wondering what I was thinking in setting that date."

Charlotte passed her admin's empty desk in the small reception area, and walked into her own office. "Did you find a dress?"

"I did. And it's being altered right now."

"That has to be a huge relief." She remembered falling in love with a gown of her own, one she'd ended up donating.

"It's beautiful. Makes me feel like a princess. Which as you know is not me at all. Anyway, enough about that." Her voice became softer. "I am calling to see if you're coming to the ceremony."

Charlotte flipped on her office light and sank into the chair behind her desk. "Honestly I wasn't planning on it. I didn't want to make things awkward for you."

"Awkward for *me*? Are you kidding?"

"I know Garrett means a lot to you and Jacob."

Elissa sighed. "He does. But…" She fell silent as if weighing her words. "Is it okay for us to talk about this?"

"About...?"

"I never wanted to be swept up in that whole thing, and I wasn't happy about it. I didn't see a way it could end well. And I know all too well what it's like to be in your shoes."

"In what way?"

"Not many people know the story of how Jacob and I actually met."

Curious, Charlotte swiveled her chair so she was looking toward the Rockies and tonight's cloudy, watercolor sunset. Night was starting to fall. Off in the distance, an office building was decorated for the holidays in festive red lights.

"He kidnapped me."

"He... *What?*"

"Literally." Elissa laughed. "He tossed me over his shoulder and threw me in his truck and drove me to his ranch."

"You've got to be kidding me!" Charlotte couldn't even picture that happening. Jacob seemed so respectful to his future wife. Then again, she recalled the subject of Elissa's painting and the intensity of the emotion in the art. Perhaps there was more to their relationship than Charlotte had guessed. "You're going to have to give me more details."

"According to Hawkeye—"

Who was in the middle of all of these messes.

"My life was in danger. Since I didn't believe him, I refused protection. Sound familiar?"

"A little."

"Jacob did what he felt he needed to in order to take care of me. Charlotte..."

She waited.

"I don't know much about your situation. But if the guys think you're in danger, you could be."

And still her father was overprotective. She understood more now that he'd told her about his medical condition, but she didn't think she was at a higher risk than she'd been before.

"And that's why I went along. I need to apologize for my part in it. I thought you wouldn't want to talk to me again."

"Oh God, no." Vehemently Charlotte shook her head. "That's not it at all, I promise. You have nothing at all to be sorry for. I promise you that."

"If I'm forgiven, I hope you'll consider coming to the wedding. It would mean a lot to me. I have a lot of respect for you personally as well as what you do for the foundation."

"I enjoyed working with you on the event." Since she'd returned to town, she'd started to realize how empty her life had become.

Since her engagement ended and she'd been ready to drown in the embarrassment, she'd become a lot like Bradley, relentlessly focused on work at the expense of everything else, including friendships.

That needed to change.

"Will you at least consider it? I can let you know if we hear from Garrett one way or another. That way you can make an informed decision. I know that I wouldn't want to be caught off guard."

"I'd appreciate that." She thought about the invitation. She'd love to see Elissa get married.

"I totally understand if you can't come. The date is really close to Christmas."

Which could be an advantage. Charlotte could still spend the holiday in Steamboat, and maybe, just maybe, she could convince her dad to join her. The heart attack had been an eye-opener for him as well. "I'll let you know for sure. But for now, mark me down as a yes."

Elissa squealed. "Seriously? This makes me *sooo* happy."

"Me too. Any excuse to get back to the ranch. In the

meantime, will you be cochair of next year's fundraising committee? I could use someone as smart as you."

"Do you mean it?" Shock echoed in Elissa voice. "Even though it means I can't do anything until next year?"

"That's when all the work begins anyway. So yes, definitely."

"In that case, I'm in."

"Good. I'll let the president know. I am looking forward to working together." And forming a real friendship. "If you're ever in Denver, I'd love to have lunch or dinner with you."

"Deborah, Mom, and I are considering a spa day before the wedding. If you can make it…"

"Let me know when." She ended the call happier than she'd been in a long time. For a few minutes, her mind had escaped from the reality of Garrett's betrayal and worry about her dad's health.

Charlotte opened her bottom desk drawer and was reaching for her purse so she could go home when her phone rang again, this time with her father's number.

Good. At least she didn't have to reach out to him. He'd told her she was worrying too much, and he'd started ignoring her calls from time to time.

With her knee, she closed the drawer, and then looked up when Bradley knocked on the doorjamb.

She struggled to hide her sigh. And no matter how hard she tried, she couldn't summon a smile. "Bradley." A few hours ago, they'd had a lunchtime meeting about making forward progress with Workflow.ai, and he'd reiterated the fact he thought they should announce their engagement soon. Again she'd been polite but firm. "What can I do for you?"

"I'm tired of this bullshit."

He took two steps into the room.

"What are you talking about?" The stench of alcohol reached her. At lunch he'd had a martini, but this was far more than a single drink.

"This is bull...*shit*."

She grabbed her phone and placed it in her jacket pocket, then gave it a quick glance to be sure she'd pushed the right button on the home screen.

He weaved his way toward her and smacked his fist against the desktop.

"You need to have a seat."

But he didn't. "I'm tired of being the nice guy."

"I was just leaving for the night. My dad's expecting me." She stood so that he wasn't looming over her. "We're planning to talk about Workflow.ai, as promised. I'll report back to you tomorrow."

"Fuck off, Charlotte."

Blinking from shock, she slowly reached toward the small button tucked next to her top drawer, but he leaped into action with shockingly fast reflexes.

Features contorted into an ugly snarl, he shoved her hard, knocking her against the credenza, the impact sucking the air from her lungs in a stabbing rush.

"Oh fuck. Look what you made me do!"

Desperately she grabbed hold of her chair so she didn't fall and so that there was a barrier between them.

But he knocked it out of the way, leaving her helpless.

"We're getting married, Charlotte." His eyes were wide and wild. "This company is mine, and you're not going to keep it from me, you stupid, stupid, spoiled little bitch." He wrapped his hands around her throat.

Desperately she snatched her phone and smashed it into the bone beneath his eye socket.

He screamed his rage, then tightened his grip.

As she clawed at his hands, the floor spun, and her knees buckled before everything went black.

CHAPTER TWELVE

HAWKEYE

Earlier

From his car across the street, Garrett watched Bradley head into the Connelly and Company office building, following an afternoon at the bar.

When Malcom Connelly called, Garrett answered immediately.

"I killed the Workflow deal."

"Does Bradley know?"

"If he doesn't, he'll know soon. And we'll have our answer."

"He's onsite." Garrett cut his car engine and climbed from behind the wheel.

"At Connelly?"

"Yeah."

"I'll let Charlotte know."

And I'll make doubly sure everything's okay.

The elevator doors closed behind Bradley, whisking him toward the top floor.

A security guard stopped Garrett. "I'll need you to sign in and show some identification, sir. What floor are you visiting?"

"Thirty-first. And I don't have time to sign in."

Malcolm called again, and his voice was frantic. "She didn't answer."

"I'm on it." He strode to the bank of elevators.

"Sir! You need to sign in, or I'll call the police."

The man was Hawkeye, and Garrett knew damn well he'd follow procedure. "You do that. And call Inamorata while you're at it." A bell dinged, indicating the car was arriving. "You've got two choices: come with me or wait for backup."

"You can't do this."

"The best accident is one that never happens." Page one of the Hawkeye training manual. The guard would recognize the motto.

Garrett entered the elevator and repeatedly jammed the button for the thirty-first floor. The doors took forever to close, and when they did, he rocketed up, leaving the guard gaping, walkie-talkie in hand.

When the compartment opened, he scanned the signage for Charlotte's office.

"Oh fuck. Look what you made me do!"

The words were followed by a sickening crash.

He sprinted down the hall, then raged in white-hot heat when he saw Bradley's hands around Charlotte's throat.

"You fucking bitch!"

"Take your goddamn hands off her!" Garrett didn't stop to reason with the son of a bitch. Instead he took advantage of the surprise, devouring the distance, ripping him away from Charlotte.

For a second she was motionless, but then she blinked and scooted back.

Barely controlling his fury, Garrett hauled back to strike Bradley's carotid artery with the side of his hand. The man's eyes rolled back, and he crumpled to the floor in a satisfying heap.

In the distance, the elevator dinged.

Despite the temptation to kick the living shit out of him and leave him for dead, Garrett bent beside Charlotte. "How bad are you hurt?"

She softly pressed her palms against her neck. "I think I'm okay."

The security guard hustled into the office. "Jesus, Ms. Connelly. Are you okay?"

Garrett shot the man a glance. "Did you call Inamorata?"

"Yes. Who the hell are you, anyway?"

"Inamorata will explain."

Bradley groaned and started to move.

"Get a pair of handcuffs on Mr. Simms. And get him the fuck out of this room." When the man didn't move, he bit out, *"Now."*

While the security guard did as instructed, Garrett crouched near Charlotte, intentionally blocking her view of her attacker.

Still, she backed up against the wall and hugged herself.

Though he ached to hold her in his arms, he gave her space, hating the fingerprints the animal had left on her.

"What the hell is going on?"

He drew a breath to steady his primal fury. His woman was the only thing that mattered. "With Bradley? It's a long story. And you probably need to hear it from your dad."

"My dad?" She blinked. "What do you know about my dad?"

"That he's a damn smart man who loves you very much." *Like I do.*

"And why are you here?"

He had practiced answers to that question, and now that the moment was here, he had nothing to say except the unvarnished truth. He may never again have the opportunity to voice these words. "I never left."

"What's that supposed to mean?"

"I fell in love with you the night of the fundraiser. At first, there was a recognition when we both bid on Elissa's painting."

She scowled.

"And then at the hotel. You were curled up in front of the fireplace, sipping champagne." He sat on the floor, near but not too close. "Then you ghosted me and earned my respect forever."

"That's absurd."

"Agree. I keep telling myself that."

In the next room, Bradley raged, indignant, insisting the handcuffs be removed.

"I fell in love with you. Your heart. Your soul."

"You stayed?" Her voice was wobbly. "Even after I fired you?"

"Yes. I meant it, Charlotte. You were never just a job to me. It was never about the money." He ached to touch her, but he didn't have that right. "I can live with your anger and hatred. But I couldn't survive if anything were to happen to you."

"Garrett…" Her blue eyes glazed with tears. "I need…"

He had to hear what she had to say.

"I need you."

Her emotional walls crumbled into a mass of shaking sobs. Murmuring promises of his everlasting protection, he went to her, gathering her onto his lap and into his arms. "If you will give me—us—another chance, I will do everything in my power to earn your trust."

She cried into his shoulder, and he held her there while her emotion and fear were cleansed.

He had no idea how much time passed until Inamorata strode into the room, perfectly calm and put together in her crisp dress shirt and pencil skirt.

Before releasing Charlotte, he met Inamorata's eyes. "Is Simms gone?"

She gave a brief no-nonsense nod.

"Can we get a medic in here?"

Charlotte shook her head. "I'm fine."

"Medic," he said.

"Garrett…"

"I'm sorry, Charlotte. Your dad will want to know you're okay." *And so will I.*

A female medic entered the room. She knelt next to Charlotte while Garrett stepped into the reception area with Inamorata.

"Well, Mr. Young. You know how to create a stir."

He shrugged.

"Care to explain yourself?"

"No." He shrugged. Since he no longer worked for Hawkeye, he owed no one an explanation.

"I'll ensure you're kept out of jail."

"You'll want a few agents to raid Simms's office. And seize his computer. Shut down his access to every part of the company."

"Already in progress."

"Since I assume your contract with Connelly and Company is still in effect, I'd like a chartered plane to take her to Steamboat."

"I'll see what I can do."

"And Torin and Mira on the job."

She sighed.

Malcolm Connelly hustled through the door, ashen and thin. "Where's Charlotte?"

Inamorata took charge, as she should. "Through here, sir."

"Dad!"

From the doorway, he watched Charlotte unsteadily climb to her feet. And the two of them hugged in tearful, laughter-filled reunion.

Garrett nodded. He'd done all he could. The rest was up to Charlotte.

Turning, he left the offices and made his way to the bank of elevators to push the call button.

"Garrett!"

As the doors parted, he stopped and looked back toward Charlotte.

"Where are you going?" She braced her hand on a wall.

"Giving you some time with your dad. You've been through a lot. I figured you'd want to process it."

"I…"

He waited.

"I love you."

Her words were simple but heartfelt.

Behind her, her dad and Inamorata stood shoulder to shoulder.

"I want us to have a second chance."

He fucking didn't deserve this. Or her. But he'd do everything in his power to make her happy.

Grinning, he went to her and cradled her in his arms, kissing her as deeply as she wanted, giving more than taking.

Once they'd stepped back from each other, Inamorata cleared her throat. "There's a plane waiting for you, Ms. Connelly."

Charlotte looked between Inamorata and Garrett.

"Per Mr. Young's request."

"You did that?"

"I figured you'd need some time up there."

The emotions in her heart radiated into her smile. "You're going with me?"

"If you'll have me."

"Saul is waiting to take you to the airport."

"Thank you." Charlotte hurried back to her dad, and they exchanged a few private words. "Promise?"

"Yes. I'll be up next week."

Garrett grinned. Things for Charlotte were looking up.

He pushed the call button again. And this time, when the doors opened, Charlotte stepped inside with him.

She backed him against the wall, and he raised an eyebrow. "Here's to our future, Mr. Young."

"Most certainly, Ms. Connelly." He pressed the Stop button and sealed his promise of forever with a searing kiss.

EPILOGUE

HAWKEYE

Two Weeks Later

Charlotte was in the ranch house bathroom, swiping on a final coat of lipstick when a movement caught her eye.

She glanced to the left to see a reflection of Garrett with one shoulder propped against the doorjamb. As their gazes met, a slow, lazy smile curved his lips.

"You look gorgeous."

Charlotte capped the tube, then dropped it into the drawer before turning to look at him. "You don't look so bad yourself, cowboy." That was an understatement. With his tailored trousers, white Western shirt, black string tie, and leather blazer, he was delicious beyond words.

"Shall we?"

They were heading to Jacob and Elissa's wedding, and they were already behind schedule. Earlier, when Garrett had seen the way her red dress hugged her curves, he'd stripped her out of the gown and spanked her until she was begging him to get her off.

Frustrating her, he told her she had to wait until they got home.

She crossed to him and straightened his tie. "You were right earlier. We could skip the wedding."

"We could." His eyes darkened. "But we won't."

"You've got an evil streak."

"Yeah." His shrug was easy. "I do."

They then descended the staircase together. Life wasn't perfect, but she was happier than she ever remembered being.

Her father's health was still a major concern. But last week he'd spent a few days up here relaxing. They'd even had dinner with Jacob and Elissa at the brewpub.

Malcolm still wanted the succession plan by the end of the year, but he told her they could consider hiring a CEO from outside the organization. Garrett had been added to the management team as head of security. In the aftermath of Bradley's attack, she learned that her dad had contacted Garrett—mostly because Malcolm knew how much Garrett meant to her.

Malcolm had tasked Garrett with looking into the LLC that invested in Workflow. Garrett had started to dig and discovered Bradley was the only real member of the LLC. Further digging into Bradley revealed deep financial problems, mostly from gambling. He'd needed to profit from the acquisition...or marry Charlotte.

The bastard was in jail awaiting trial thanks to the recording that Charlotte had made during his attack.

Downstairs, Garrett helped her into her jacket. "I'm the luckiest man on the planet."

She turned to kiss him. "I love you."

Once they were in the car, she chose a radio station that

played jazzy Christmas songs.

"Again?"

She nodded. "Every day until the new year."

He groaned.

"I could change it to pop Christmas if you prefer. We can listen to "Santa Baby' again."

Vehemently he shook his head.

"Or how about 'Jingle Bell Rock'?"

"Jazz is fine."

She grinned. "I thought you'd see it my way."

Still shaking his head, he pushed a button on the steering wheel. "Snow Queen on the move."

"You and your secret agent stuff."

"Come on. Confess the truth." He slid her a glance. "You find it sexy."

"Maybe just a little."

Though she still wasn't comfortable with having security around, she was more accepting of it now. Bradley's arrest had put the family back in the news, and the search for a CEO would hit the press soon.

She did like the new Hawkeye team that Garrett had brought on to replace Torin and Mira, even if she thought Garrett was being overprotective. After Bradley's attack, it had taken Garrett a week to make love to her, and it was only in the last couple of days that he'd spanked her again.

At Jacob's ranch, a valet greeted them and opened their doors.

Waffle apparently considered herself part of the greeting committee, and she wove her way around Charlotte's legs.

"Finicky feline."

As if knowing Garrett was talking about her, Waffle looked up at him. This time, she didn't hiss. Instead, she flicked her tail and walked off.

"I think she's warming up to me."

Charlotte laughed as she turned over her coat to a hired attendant. "None of us ladies can resist your charms for long."

Jacob came over to greet them, shaking Garrett's hand and giving Charlotte a gentle hug. "There's a champagne fountain."

"Sounds good."

He leaned in closer to Garrett and raised a hand as if telling a secret. "The harder stuff is stashed in my office. Don't tell Elissa I said anything."

They both laughed as Jacob left them to greet newcomers.

The whole house was decorated in festive bells and streamers and bouquets of fresh-cut flowers. The kitchen and dining room were laden with ridiculous amounts of foods, and numerous chafing dishes kept hot dishes warm.

In the corner was a tall woman with her back to them, and she stood near a man.

"Not sure if this is someone you'll want to meet," Garrett said against her ear, uncertainty tingeing his words.

The woman turned, and Charlotte flashed back to the horrible night in her office. "Inamorata."

"And Hawkeye."

Charlotte exhaled deeply. "The question is, do you want to talk to them?"

"I'm fine with it."

"Since you're now their boss." She grinned.

"I hadn't looked at it that way."

"If they piss you off, just fire them. We'll hire someone else."

"Ms. Connelly." Inamorata offered her hand when they arrived. "How nice to see you." She nodded to Garrett.

Hawkeye smiled and extended his hand as well. "A pleasure to finally meet you."

He was stunning. Broad but lithe. Weary beyond his

years. But it was his eyes that captivated her. The depths were haunted as if he'd seen things no man ever should.

"I hope we'll be doing business for years to come."

She brought up her chin. "That's entirely up to Garrett."

Hawkeye nodded as he and Garrett exchanged glances. "Understood."

Mira and Torin arrived, and Charlotte gave Mira a hug.

"I was afraid you wouldn't want to have anything to do with me."

Charlotte squeezed the woman's hands reassuringly. "You were doing your job—trying to protect me. I'm grateful. But I understand you're no longer assigned to my detail."

"We're heading back to Nevada to the training center." She looked at Torin. "And we're settling into our house. First Christmas together."

"That sounds special."

As if aware of the conversation, Garrett stroked his fingers across her shoulder.

It would be their first Christmas at the ranch too.

At that moment, Mr. and Mrs. Conroy came over, shattering the tension with their joy-filled hugs and greetings. "We're so grateful you're here. It means the world to Elissa."

"We wouldn't have missed it."

"Would you like to see her?" Mrs. Conroy asked Charlotte. "She's in the bedroom getting dressed, but I know she'd love it if you peeked in."

"Really?"

"Oh yes." She nodded. "Come with me."

"Go ahead." Garrett smiled. "I'll catch up with Hawkeye and Inamorata."

"If you're sure?"

He inclined his head. "Yes."

Excited, Charlotte followed Mrs. Conroy up the stairs.

Before entering, she knocked, then cracked the door open.

Inside was a flurry of activity. Deborah was tightening the laces on the back of Elissa's gown while a photographer snapped dozens of pictures.

When she saw Charlotte, Elissa grinned, and they exchanged air hugs. "Thank you for coming."

"As I told your mom, I wouldn't have missed your special day."

Adele, Deborah's daughter, sat in a chair, swinging her legs back and forth while playing with a basket of rose petals.

It was difficult to imagine anything more perfect than this, even if they'd had months to organize the event.

The wedding planner entered the room, an electronic tablet in hand. "Five minutes."

Among the gasps and squeals, Charlotte slipped away to rejoin Garrett. Thoughtfully he was holding her coat so that she wouldn't freeze when they were outside.

Numerous heaters blazed, not that they were needed. The afternoon couldn't have been more beautiful, with cerulean skies bathed in sunshine.

Wedding music drifted from unseen speakers.

A minister exited the house, followed down the red-carpeted aisle by Hawkeye and Jacob, both now wearing black felt cowboy hats.

When they were standing in front of the arch that had been set up at the far end of the patio, Elissa's parents made their way to seats in the front. Then came Adele who tossed rose petals as she skipped along.

Then the "Wedding March" began, and the minister asked everyone to stand for the bride.

Upstairs, Elissa had been beyond beautiful, and now she was radiant. Her gown sparkled in the sunlight, and her focus seemed intent on her husband.

When she neared him, Jacob took her hands and raised one to his lips. Then he swept her into his arms and kissed her deeply.

The minister chuckled, then cleared his throat. "I believe you've got the order of events wrong, Jacob."

Undaunted, and among the cheers and whistles from the guests, he kissed his future bride until he was ready to let her go.

"Sorry." Though he nodded to the minister, his grin was completely unapologetic.

Elissa and Jacob exchanged the vows that they'd each written, a promise to the future that they would unravel together one day at a time.

"I now pronounce you husband and wife." The minister closed his book. "You may kiss your bride… again."

This time, he took off his cowboy hat and held it in front of them to offer a little privacy as he kissed her.

"Ladies and gentlemen, I present Mr. And Mrs. Walker."

As people clapped, Jacob gave his hat to Hawkeye.

Elissa gasped when Jacob lifted her from the ground and tossed her over his shoulder where she landed with a laughing squeal. "Jacob!" She beat on his back.

"We're starting this marriage as I intend to go on." He carried her back up the aisle and into the house.

The minister stood there shaking his head.

It was certainly the most unusual ceremony Charlotte had attended, and maybe the funniest too.

After the food was served, a DJ started through the bride's requested playlist of dance songs and ballads.

A late arrival made Garrett smile. "Charlotte, I'd like you to meet my brother-in-arms, Kane Anderson."

He tipped his hat to her. "A pleasure, ma'am."

Beyond that, he didn't say much, and he kept to himself.

On the way home she asked about him. "He looks dangerous."

Garrett slid her a glance. "Depends who you are."

When they neared her home—their home—he tapped the app button on the car's screen.

"What's that?"

"Hello, Holly."

"Are you…" She'd heard of Julien Bonds's fully integrated AI system, named Hello, Molly. It could be customized for each user so that everyone had a unique experience.

With a grin, he spoke to the computer. "Hello, Holly. Open gate and disarm house alarm."

"My pleasure."

"See? Isn't it handy having an app?"

Charlotte rolled her eyes. "It would be useful if she could brew coffee for us."

"I can do that."

"You can?" Was she really talking to a computer?

"Most certainly. Would you like it ready at a specific time or would you like to let me know each day?"

Charlotte and Garrett exchanged glances. "Okay. Now I'm convinced."

He shrugged. "Who knew you could be bought so easily?"

The car screen had a flashing light on it. "I'll let you know each day, Holly."

"Very good, ma'am."

As they neared the house, lights came on, making it appear warm and inviting. Why had she been so resistant to this technology?

Once they were inside, Garrett closed the door, and the lock automatically slid into place. "I've been having a thought…"

"Have you?"

"About paddling you next to the Christmas tree."

The desire that had been on simmer now boiled inside her. "Have you been reading my mind, Sir?"

He helped her from her coat and hung it in the closet before tossing his hat onto a nearby table. His eyes darkened. "Go get your wooden paddle."

Finally.

"And come back naked."

Shivers danced up her spine.

Instead of waiting for her in the great room, he met her at the bottom of the stairs and guided her to the couch.

"How many days have we waited for this?"

"Too many, Sir."

"Ten? Twelve?"

She sucked in a breath. "Maybe fifteen."

"Then that's the number of paddles you'll receive."

Charlotte surrendered to his kiss, one that aroused her completely. He told the computer to turn on the fireplace, then fondled her breasts as the flames created an intimate atmosphere.

She groaned when he sucked on her nipples and played with her pussy. Hunger consumed her. "Please."

Like the first night, he sat on the couch, then extended a hand for the paddle that he placed near him on the table. Then he helped her into position—her torso flat on the cushions, her ass on his lap.

"How many, again?"

"Fifteen, Sir."

Before starting, he rubbed her skin hard to bring the blood flow to the area. Then he began to wield the paddle, soft at first, maybe because it had been so long. After he passed five, he increased the intensity and the speed. Each fell with a hollow rhythm that seemed to envelop her.

Too soon he was done, and every part of her craved his possession.

Whispering words of love, he helped her to stand, and she sank to her knees to release his belt buckle and open his pants.

He grabbed a condom they'd stashed in the end table drawer, and she rolled the protection into place before straddling him and welcoming his cock inside her heat.

This was perfect.

They breathed together, had sex, made love until their movements were in unison. Together. Forever.

He played with her, caressing her clit until she shattered once, then twice before taking his own orgasm.

Afterward he took her upstairs and made love to her slowly, worshiping every inch of her body. He moved his head between her legs and licked, bringing her off again before sitting up in the bed and pulling her next to him.

With the full moon outside the window and a star twinkling nearby, he angled himself so that he could look her in the eyes. Then he clasped her shoulders. "Charlotte Connelly, will you marry me?"

"What?" She couldn't have possibly heard him correctly.

"I'm asking if you'll do me the honor of being my wife."

Tears swam in her eyes. "Are you…? Do you mean it?"

"This isn't romantic at all. Is it?" He grimaced a little. "This isn't the way I was planning to do it. But I couldn't wait. Let me try again."

"No." She shook her head. "Don't. This is…perfect. I couldn't imagine anything better."

That's what love was to her, messy, flawed. Wonderful. Just like the relationship they'd shared from the beginning.

"You deserve better." He climbed from the bed in all his magnificent, masculine glory. His cock was already half hard.

Tugging the sheet up to keep warm, she watched him cross the room to open a dresser drawer. He returned with one hand behind his back.

He helped her from the bed, and she stood in front of him wearing nothing at all.

More uncertain than she'd ever seen her badass man look, he lowered himself to one knee and opened a tiny box.

The ring stole her breath. "It's…" Emotion overtook her.

"Your mother's ring."

"Oh my God. How…?"

"Your dad gave it to me."

She blinked away the tears of joy and tried in vain to swallow the knot in her throat. "So you asked him?"

"I knew his blessing would matter to you, so it mattered to me. He brought it with him when he came to visit us."

"Garrett Young, just when I thought I couldn't love you more, you do this." Tears spilled down her cheeks.

He sought her gaze, then he took one of her hands. "Charlotte, please tell me you'll marry me."

"Yes."

He slipped the ring into place.

"This is the most amazing moment I could have ever dreamed of. My mom would have loved you like I do."

"I love you today, tomorrow, forever. I will do my best to earn your love and respect every day."

He slid the ring onto her finger. The fit was perfect, and she moved her hand a hundred directions, admiring the way it sparkled in the moonlight.

"Uhm, there's one little detail…"

She frowned.

"Your dad asked me to mention the succession plan."

"Are you kidding me right now?" Charlotte shook her head.

"Something about getting started on giving him grandchildren right away."

In pure delight, she laughed.

With a grin, he lifted her back onto the bed. "Shall we get started on that plan right away?"

"Yes." She surrendered to her future husband and the happiness they intended to create together.

◊ ◊ ◊ ◊ ◊

Thank you for reading Believe in Me. I hope you loved Charlotte and Garrett's story. This is one I've wanted to tell for years. I always had a sense of who Charlotte was, but it took me a while to figure out Garrett. He's so protective, and good at his job, and even more loyal than I imagined. He's one of my favorite heroes, and I fell in love with him from his first interaction with Hawkeye. Garrett's sense of integrity and humor enchanted me from the beginning.

You can read more about the dangerous and irresistible cowboy, Jacob, in Hold On To Me.

He was supposed to protect her, not fall in love.

Sexy cowboy Jacob Carter has one last mission for Hawkeye Security: keeping Elissa Conroy safe from a madman…even if it means kidnapping her and guarding her beautiful body twenty-four hours a day.

Discover Hold On To Me

For Torin and Mira's story, I invite you to read Meant For Me. As his trainee, Mira was far too young and much too innocent for Torin's carnal demands. And now she's been assigned as his partner, placing her firmly in the forbidden category.

Even though she hated him for pushing her so hard during training, Mira has always been attracted to the older, sexy-as-sin Hawkeye commander.

Even though danger swirls around them, Mira is a temptation Torin can't resist.

★★★★★ "The sexual tension built and built until it threatened to explode." —Bookbub Review

Discover Meant For Me

Turn the page for an exciting excerpt from HOLD ON TO ME

HOLD ON TO ME

CHAPTER ONE

"No fucking way, Hawkeye." In case that wasn't clear enough, Jacob Walker tipped back the brim of his cowboy hat and leveled a stare at his friend and former commander across the small, rickety table that separated them.

The stench of cheap whiskey and loneliness hung in the air—as putrid as it was familiar.

Through the years, they'd held dozens of meetings at this kind of place. Didn't matter which fucked-up hellhole they were in—Central America, the Middle East, Texas, or here, a small, all but forgotten Colorado mountain town, a place with no security cameras, where neither of them were known.

As usual, Hawkeye dressed to blend in with the locals—jeans, scuffed boots, and a heavyweight canvas jacket that could be found on almost every ranch in the state. He'd added a baseball cap with a logo of a tractor company embroidered on the front. Today, he also wore a beard. No doubt it would be gone within an hour of his walking back outside into the crisp, clean air.

At one time, Jacob thrived on clandestine meetings. The anticipation alone was enough to feed adrenaline into his veins, and he lived for the vicarious thrill.

But life was different now.

After a final, fateful job in Colombia that left an American businessman's daughter dead, Jacob walked away from Hawkeye Security.

He returned to the family ranch and a world he no longer recognized. His grandfather had died, no doubt from the stress of managing the holdings by himself. Though Jacob's grandmother never uttered a critical word, he knew she was disappointed that he'd missed the funeral. He wasn't even in the same country when he was needed the most.

When she passed, he stood alone at the graveside, the only family mourner, like she'd no doubt been a few years before.

Spurred by equal measures of guilt and regret, he poured himself into managing the family's holdings as a way to redeem himself. Then, because of his loneliness and the horrible dreams after Colombia, he did it as a way to save himself.

"The op will take less than a month." Hawkeye shrugged. "Give or take. I'll give you three of our best agents—Johnson, Laurents, Mansfield. You can man the gate, rather than just utilizing the speaker box. Another on perimeter. One for relief. You have the space and a bunkhouse."

Jacob shook his head to clear it of the ever-present memories. "Is there a part of my refusal that you don't understand?" Of course there was. When Hawkeye wanted something, nothing would dissuade him. That willful determination had made him a force on the battlefield as well as in the business arena. "When I quit, I meant it." He took a swig from his longneck beer bottle. "No regrets." The words were mostly true. There were times he wanted the camaraderie and wanted to flex his brain as well as his muscles. There was also the sweet thrill of the hunt. And making things right in the world.

Rather than argue, Hawkeye removed his cap long enough for Jacob to get a look at his former boss. Worry lines were trenched between his eyebrows. In all his years, Jacob had never seen dark despair in those eyes. "Yesterday, Inamorata received what appeared to be a birthday card from her sister."

Ms. Inamorata was Hawkeye's right-hand woman and known for her ability to remain calm under duress. She could be counted on to deal with local and federal authorities, smoothing over all the details. Rather seriously, Hawkeye said she batted cleanup better than any major leaguer.

Jacob told himself to stand up, thank Hawkeye for the drink, then get the hell out of here while he still could. Instead, he remained where he was.

"There was a white powder inside."

Jesus. "Anthrax?"

"Being tested. She took appropriate precautions and received immediate medical assistance. Antibiotics were prescribed as a precaution." Hawkeye paused. "There were no warning signs that the piece of mail was suspicious."

Meaning the postmark matched the return address. The postage amount was correct, and there was nothing protruding from the envelope.

Jacob knew Inamorata and liked her as much as he respected her. He took offense at a threat to her life. "Received at headquarters?"

"No. At her home. So whoever sent it has access to information about her and how to circumvent our protocols."

Slowly he nodded. "Any message?"

"Yeah." Hawkeye paused. "Threats to take out people I care about, one at a time."

"The fuck?" Instead of sympathizing, Jacob switched to ops mode. He didn't do it on purpose—it was as immediate as it was instinctive. No doubt Hawkeye had counted on Jacob's reaction. "Anything else?"

"There was no specific request. No signature." Hawkeye paused. "I've got profilers taking a look at it. But there's not much to go on. Tech is analyzing writing and sentence structure, tracking down places the card could have come from. FBI has the powder at its lab. Profilers are trying to ascertain the type of person most likely to behave this way."

All the right things.

"But we don't have the resources to take care of our clients and have eyes on everyone who's a potential target."

At this point, there was no way to know how serious the threat was. A card was one thing, a physical attack was another.

"I don't give a fuck who comes for me."

Over the years, their line of work—cleaning up situations to keep secrets safe, protecting people and precious objects, even acting as paramilitary support operators overseas—had created a long list of enemies.

"But I can't risk the people I care about." Hawkeye reached into a pocket inside his jacket and pulled out a picture. "I need you to take care of her."

"Oh fuck no, man." Jacob could be a sounding board, analyze data, but he didn't have the time to return to babysitting services.

Undeterred, Hawkeye continued. "Her name's Elissa. Elissa Conroy. Twenty-eight. My plan was to have Agent Fagen move in with her and accompany her to work."

Makes logical sense. "And?"

"She refused. Then I decided I'd prefer for her to be away

from Denver, out of her normal routine in case anyone has been watching." After a moment's hesitation, Hawkeye slid the snapshot onto the table, facedown.

Hawkeye knew every one of Jacob's weaknesses. If he glanced at Elissa's face, the job would become personal. She wouldn't be a random woman he could ignore.

Jacob looked across the expanse of the room, at the two men talking trash at the nearby pool table. Above them, a neon beer sign dangled from a tired-looking nail. The paint was peeling from the shabby wall, and the red glare from the light made the atmosphere all the more depressing.

"Her parents own a pub. Right now, she's running it on their behalf while they're back home in Ireland for a well-deserved vacation. Her father has just recovered from a bout with cancer, and they're celebrating his recovery."

Of course Hawkeye crafted a compelling narrative. He knew how to motivate people, be it through their heartstrings or sense of justice. At times, he'd stoke anger. His ability to get people to do what he wanted was his biggest strength as well as his greatest failing.

Never had his powers of persuasion been more on display than when he'd gotten his Army Ranger team out of Peru, despite the overwhelming odds.

From the beginning, the mission had been FUBAR—fucked up beyond all recognition. They sustained enough casualties to decimate even the strongest and bravest. Relentlessly Hawkeye had urged each soldier on. Despite his own injuries, Hawkeye had carried one man miles to the extraction point.

What happened immediately after that would haunt Hawkeye and Jacob to the end of their days, and it created a bond each would take to the grave.

"You've had some time on the ranch. I assume you're a hundred percent?"

Physically, yes. But part of him would always be in that South American jungle, trying to figure out what had gone so horribly fucking wrong.

Hawkeye nudged the photograph a little closer to Jacob.

"Who is she to you?"

Hawkeye hesitated long enough to capture Jacob's interest.

"Someone I used to know."

Jacob studied his friend intently. "Used to?"

Hawkeye shrugged. "It was a long time ago. Right after we got back from Peru." He stared at the photo. "She helped me through the rough patch."

Tension made Hawkeye's voice rough, and he cleared his throat.

"Shit." Jacob cursed himself for not walking out the moment Hawkeye asked for help. "It—whatever it was between you—is in the past?"

"Yeah. She's a smart woman, recognized damaged goods and was astute enough not to follow when I walked away." He shrugged. "To tell the truth, she's too damn good for me. We both knew it."

"It's over?"

"There never was anything significant. She's a friend. Nothing more. But if anyone's intent on hurting me…" With great deliberation, Hawkeye flipped over the picture.

Jacob couldn't help himself. He looked.

The woman was breathtaking. She was seated on a white-painted carousel horse, arms wrapped around its shiny brass pole. Dark, wavy hair teased her shoulders. But it was her eyes that stopped him cold.

He was a practical man more accustomed to making life-and-death decisions than indulging in fanciful poetry, but that particular shade of blue made him think of the columbines that carpeted the ranch's meadow each summer.

Her smile radiated a joy that he wasn't sure he'd ever experienced. Longing—hot and swift—ripped through him. Ruthlessly he shoved the unfamiliar emotion away. He was seated across from Hawkeye, discussing a job. Nothing more. If he accepted the assignment, it would be his responsibility to keep her safe and ensure she had plenty to smile about in the future.

"After this, Commander Walker, we'll call it even."

"Even from you, that's a fucking cheap shot." Jacob didn't need the reminder of how much he owed Hawkeye. Nothing would ever be *even* after the way the man rescued Jacob's mother from the inside of a Mexican jail cell.

Unable to stop himself, Jacob picked up the photo. Hawkeye's gamble—his drive deep into the Colorado mountains—had paid off. Jacob couldn't walk away. Elissa wasn't a random client. She was a woman who'd shown compassion to Hawkeye, and that shouldn't have put her at risk.

With a silent vow that he'd care for her until the shitstorm passed, Jacob tucked the picture inside his shirt pocket.

Hawkeye lifted his shot glass, then downed his whiskey in a single swallow.

"Sir? It's closing time." Elissa summoned a false, I'm-not-exhausted smile for the cowboy sitting alone at a table for two in her mom and dad's Denver-area pub. The man had been there for hours, his back to the wall. From time to time, he'd glance at the baseball game on the television, but for the most part, he watched other customers coming and going. More than once, she was aware of his focused gaze on her as she worked.

When he arrived, he asked for a soda water with lime.

Nothing stronger. Minutes before the kitchen closed, he ordered the pub's famous fish and chips.

Throughout the evening, he hadn't engaged with her attempts at conversation, and he paid his bill—in cash, with a generous tip—before last call.

Now he was the last remaining customer, and she wanted him to leave so she could lock up, head for home. She needed a long, hot bath, doused with a generous helping of her favorite lavender Epsom salts.

If she were lucky, she'd fall asleep quickly and manage a few hours of deep sleep before the alarm shrieked, dragging her out of bed. After all, she still had to run her own business while taking care of the bar.

Over the past few days, exhaustion had made her mentally plan a vacation, far away from Colorado. Maybe a remote tropical island where she could rest and bask in the sun. A swim-up bar would be nice, and so would a beachside massage beneath a palm tree.

But she was still stuck in reality. She had to complete the closing checklist, and that meant dispensing with the final, reluctant-to-leave guest.

With a forced half smile, she tried again. "Sir?"

The man tipped the brim of his cowboy hat, allowing her to get a good look at his face.

She pressed her hand to her mouth to stifle a gasp.

He was gorgeous. Not just classically handsome, but drop-dead, movie star gorgeous.

His square jaw was shadowed with stubble, but that enhanced the sharpness of his features. And his eyes… They were bright green, reminding her of a malachite gemstone she'd seen in a tourist shop.

In a leisurely perusal, he swept his gaze up her body, starting with her sensible shoes, then moving up her thighs, taking in the curve of her hips, then the swell of her suddenly aching breasts.

When their gazes met, she was helplessly ensnared, riveted by his intensity.

The silence stretched, and she cleared her throat. She was usually a total professional, accustomed to dealing with loners, as well as groups out celebrating and being rowdy, or even the occasional customer in search of a therapist while drowning their sorrows. But this raw, physical man left her twitterpated, her pulse racing while her imagination soared on hungry, sexual wings.

Andrew, the barback, switched off some of the lights, jolting her. After shaking her head, she asserted herself. "It's closing time, sir."

"Yes, ma'am." The cowboy stood, the legs of his chair scraping against the wooden floor. "I'll be going, then."

His voice was deep and rich, resonating through her. It invited trust even as it hinted at intimacy.

An involuntary spark of need raced up her spine.

Forcing herself to ignore it, she followed him to the exit. Instead of leaving, he paused.

They stood so close that she inhaled his scent, that of untamed open spaces. She tried to move away but was rooted to the spot. She was ensnared by his masculine force field—an intoxicating mixture of raw dominance and constrained power.

Desire lay like smoke in his eyes. In a response as old as time, pheromones stampeded through her. She ached to know him, to feel his strong arms wrap around her, to have his hips grinding against hers as he claimed her hard.

Dear God, what is wrong with me?

It had been too long since she'd been with a lover, but this cowboy was the type of man who'd turn her inside out if she let him. And she was too smart for that.

"Ma'am." Finally he thumbed the brim of his hat in a casual, respectful farewell that made her wonder if she'd imagined what had just happened between them.

"Thanks for coming in." Her response was automatic.

"I'll see you soon." Conviction as well as promise laced his words, and it shocked her how much she hoped he meant it.

After locking the door behind him, she stood in place for a few moments, watching him climb into his nondescript black pickup truck. It resembled a thousand others on the road, in stark contrast to its intense, unforgettable owner.

The barback tugged the chain to turn off the Open sign, reminding her of the chores still ahead of her.

It was past time to shove away thoughts of the stranger.

She checked her watch. A few minutes after one a.m.

It had been a long day. *Another* long day. With her parents still on vacation, the responsibility for running the pub had fallen to her. That wouldn't have been so bad, but Mary, the nighttime manager, had called in sick. And Elissa's freelance graphic project was due at the end of the week. Sleep had been in short supply for the past month.

Month?

Actually, it had been more than a year. Her father's cancer diagnosis had upended her family's world. The emotional turmoil had taken its toll as they all fought through the terrifying uncertainty and fear.

After his final chemotherapy treatment, her parents had departed for a much-needed break.

Andrew continued walking through the area, switching off the neon beer signs. "Everything's done. Clean and ready for tomorrow."

"Not sure how I would have managed without you." For the first time ever, he'd ended up waiting on several customers, and he'd done a good job. "Why don't you go ahead and leave?"

"I'll wait until you're done and walk you to your car."

"That's okay." She shook her head. It had been busier than usual for a Tuesday, more like she'd expect closer to the weekend. "I still have to reconcile the cash register, and that will take some time. You worked your ass off this evening. Go see your girlfriend."

"It's our one-month date-iversary. I didn't know that was a thing until this morning, and she warned me I better not screw it up." Clearly besotted, he grinned. "I don't mind staying, though, for a few more minutes."

"Go."

He glanced toward the rear exit. "If you're sure…"

"It's your date-iversary. *Go.*" She made a sweeping motion with her hand.

Grinning, she turned the deadbolt once he left.

After turning off the main dining room lights, Elissa retreated to the tiny management office. She sank into the old military-surplus style leather chair behind the metal desk. Determined to ignore the clock on the wall, she counted the cash, balanced the register, then ran the credit card settlement.

Once everything was done and the bank deposit was locked in the safe, she sighed, part in relief, part in satisfaction.

Finally.

As usual, she straightened the desktop and gave the office a final glance to be sure everything was where it needed to be.

Satisfied, she released her hair from its ponytail and fed her fingers through the strands to separate them, part of her ritual for ending the workday and easing into her off time.

Then she reached for her lightweight jacket. Even though it was summer, Colorado could still hold a chill after the sun set. Finally she slung her purse over her shoulder before plucking her keyring from a hook in the wall.

She let herself out the door, then secured the deadbolt behind her.

There were only a handful of vehicles in the parking lot, and she headed toward hers at a quick clip.

As she neared it, a figure detached itself from the adjoining building.

She struggled for calm, telling herself that the person wasn't heading toward her. But as she broke into a jog, so did the figure.

Frantically she ran, hitting the remote control to unlock the car, praying she could make it to safety before the assailant reached her. As she grasped the door handle, he crowded behind her, pressing her against the side of the vehicle.

"Get away from me!"

When he didn't, she screamed.

"Calm down."

Fuck. She recognized his gruff voice. *The cowboy.* For a moment, she went still. But when he pressed her harder against the car, fear flared, and she instinctively fought back. "Get the hell off me!"

He was unyielding, and her strength was no match for his.

"Hawkeye sent me."

Elissa froze. *Hawkeye?*

Of course he'd sent someone. She should have expected it when she refused to let him provide her with a bodyguard.

Years before, she'd met the wounded military man when he returned from an overseas mission. The first few times he'd come into the pub, he'd been quiet, drinking whiskey neat, staring at a wall while occasionally flinching.

They'd gone out a number of times, and she'd cared about

him. But no matter how hard she tried, she couldn't connect with him on an emotional level. He kept more secrets than he shared. But the one thing she learned was that the need for revenge consumed his every waking thought. In the end, it had been impossible to have any kind of relationship with him.

When he informed her that he'd started Hawkeye Security, she wasn't surprised. And when he came to say goodbye, she tearfully stroked his cheek while wishing him well.

She had been stunned when he called her to tell her she was at risk. Someone from his past threatened the people he cared about. Before hanging up, she dismissed his ridiculous concerns. Their halfhearted relationship was so far in the past that no one could possibly believe that she meant anything to Hawkeye.

"You're going to need to come with me."

"Oh hell no." Her earlier attraction to the stranger had vanished, replaced by anger. She made her own choices and didn't appreciate his heavy-handed tactics. "Tell Hawkeye I said both of you should fuck off. Or better yet, I will."

"I'm not sure you understand." His breath was warm and threatening next to her ear.

And now she understood why he'd spent so many hours at that table. He'd been studying her, planning the best way to bend her to his will.

But Elissa answered to no man.

"You're in danger."

"I can take care of myself. Now get off me, you…" *What?* "Oaf."

"As soon as you give me your word that you'll get in my truck without creating a fuss."

Realizing physical resistance was futile, she allowed her body to go limp and concentrated on tamping down her adrenaline long enough to outwit him. She needed to think and escape his unbearable presence. "How about I'll go home and stay there?"

"Not happening."

"Look..." There was no way she would yield to this oversize, determined goon, even if he was pure masculine perfection. "I'll agree to have one of his employees stay with me."

"He made that offer. You turned it down."

Damn you both. Why hadn't she just agreed to Hawkeye's suggestions?

"Let me be clear, Elissa..."

Despite herself, the way he said her name, gently curled around the sibilant sound, made her nerves tingle.

"He made it my job to protect you, and he signed off on my plan."

"Care to fill me in?"

"Yeah. We'll go to my ranch until he gives the all-clear."

Unnerved, she shivered. "Ranch?" That was worse than she could have imagined, and fresh panic set in. "I demand to talk to Hawkeye this instant."

"Demand all you want, little lady."

She refused to leave town, the pub, and be somewhere remote for an indeterminate amount of time with the cowboy shadowing her twenty-four seven. "No. No." She shook her head. "It's impossible. I'm needed here. And Hawkeye knows it." Struggling for breath, she pushed back against him. "We can work something out, I'm sure."

"You can take it up with him."

"Now we're getting somewhere. Let me get my phone out of my purse." *And figure out how to get in my car and drive like hell.*

"Not until we're on the road." He looped his massive hands around her much smaller wrists and drew them behind her.

"Ouch! Release me immediately!"

Though he didn't hurt her, his grip was uncompromising. "As soon as you agree to get in my truck without struggling."

"Look, Mr.—" *God. I don't know your name.* And like the asshole he was, he didn't fill in the missing information.

"We're done talking."

She stamped her foot on his instep, and he didn't even grunt, frustrating the hell out of her.

"Please get in my truck, Elissa."

Since he was immovable, she tried another approach, pleading with his better self. "I'm begging you. Don't do this. Let me go home." Elissa turned her head, trying to see him over her shoulder. Because of his hat and the darkness of the moonless and cloud-filled sky, his expression was unreadable. "You can follow me to my place." The lie easily rolled off her tongue. Anything to get away.

"Within the next five seconds, you'll be given two options, Ms. Conroy. One, you can come with me willingly."

"And the other?"

"You can come with me unwillingly."

"Option C. None of the above." With all her might, she shoved back, but he tightened his grip to the point of hurting her.

As if on cue, a big black truck—his, no doubt—pulled into view. Since he didn't react, it obviously meant Hawkeye had sent more than one person to deal with her. "This is absurd."

The vehicle, with no lights on, pulled to a stop nearby.

"I'll need your keys, Ms. Conroy."

She shook her head in defiance.

"Always going to do things the hard way?"

Since he was still holding her wrists, it was ridiculously easy for him to pry apart her fingers and take the fob from her.

"Has anyone ever told you that you're annoying as hell?"

A woman slid from the cab of the still-running pickup

and left the driver's side door open a crack. A gentle chime echoed around them, while light spilled from the interior, allowing Elissa to make out a few of the new arrival's features.

Dressed all in black, she was about the same height and build as Elissa. She even had long dark hair.

"Perimeter is still clear." Then in a cheery voice, she went on. "I see you haven't lost your way with the ladies, Commander."

He growled, all alpha male and frustration. "You're here to help, Fagan."

"That's exactly what I'm doing."

The cowboy eased his hold a little.

"Sorry for the caveman's actions, ma'am. I'm Agent Kayla Fagan. And I'm afraid Commander Walker needs a remedial training class in diplomacy."

Walker. First name? Or last? "Diplomacy? Is that what you call an abduction?"

He remained implacable. "I have my orders, and Ms. Conroy wasn't interested in talking."

Bastard. "His behavior needs to be reported to Hawkeye."

"I'll let you do that yourself," Kayla replied. "But honestly, I'd like to listen in."

"Get out of here, Fagan." He kept his body against hers while somehow managing to toss her keys to Kayla.

"Wait! You look so much like me you could be my double."

"That's the plan. Fagan will make it appear as if you're following your normal routine this evening while we get away. When we're on the road, you can talk to Hawkeye and make a strategic plan for opening the bar." Walker's tone was uncompromising.

The infuriating men had planned out everything.

Kayla opened the car door and slid into the driver's seat.

"Time's up, ma'am."

"Could you be any more condescending?"

"As I said, we can do this the hard way or the easy way. Your choice."

Determinedly Elissa set her chin. "I'm not going with you."

In a move so calculated and fast that she had no time to react, he took her purse from her, then yanked her around to face him. As if he'd done it a million times, he swept her off her feet, then hauled her into the air.

The Neanderthal tossed her over his shoulder, and she landed against his rigid body with so much force that breath rushed out of her lungs, stunning her into silence.

"The hard way it is."

ABOUT THE AUTHOR

HAWKEYE

I invite you to be the very first to know all the news by subscribing to my very special **VIP Reader Newsletter**! You'll find exclusive excerpts, bonus reads, and insider information.

https://www.sierracartwright.com/subscribe

For tons of fun and to join with other awesome people like you, join my Facebook reader group: **Sierra's Super Stars**

https://www.facebook.com/groups/SierrasSuperStars

And for a current booklist, please visit my **website**.

http://www.sierracartwright.com

USA Today bestselling author Sierra Cartwright was born in England, and she spent her early childhood traipsing through castles and dreaming of happily-ever afters. She has two wonderful kids and four amazing grand-kitties. She now calls Galveston, Texas home and loves to connect with her readers. Please do drop her a note.

ALSO BY SIERRA CARTWRIGHT

Titans

Sexiest Billionaire

Billionaire's Matchmaker

Billionaire's Christmas

Determined Billionaire

Scandalous Billionaire

Ruthless Billionaire

Billionaire's Revenge

Titans Quarter

His to Claim

His to Love

His to Cherish

Titans Quarter Holidays

His Christmas Gift

His Christmas Wish

His Christmas Wife

Titans Sin City

Hard Hand

Slow Burn

All-In

Titans Captivated (Ménages)

Theirs to Hold

Theirs to Love
Theirs to Wed
Theirs to Treasure

Titans: Reserve

Tease Me

Hawkeye

Come to Me
Trust in Me
Meant For Me
Hold On To Me
Believe in Me

Hawkeye: Denver

Initiation
Temptation
Determination

Bonds

Crave
Claim
Command

Donovan Dynasty

Bind
Brand
Boss

Mastered

With This Collar

On His Terms

Over The Line

In His Cuffs

For The Sub

In The Den

Collections

Titans Series

Titans Billionaires: Firsts

Titans Billionaires: Volume 1

Titans Billionaires: Volume 2

Billionaires' Quarter: Titans Quarter Collection

Risking It All: Titans Sin City Collection

Yours to Love: Titans Captivated Collection

His Christmas Temptation: Titans: Quarter Holidays

Hawkeye Series

Undercover Seduction: Hawkeye Firsts

Here for Me: Volume One

Beg For Me: Volume Two

Run, Beautiful, Run: Hawkeye Denver Collection

Made in the USA
Monee, IL
31 March 2025